D0066003

The Other Side of the Game

The Other Side of the Game

ANITA DOREEN DIGGS

KENSINGTON PUBLISHING CORP.

DAFINA BOOKS are published by

Kensington Publishing Corp.
850 Third Avenue
New York, NY 10022

Dafina Books and the Dafina logo Reg. U.S. Pat. & TM Off.

ISBN 0-7394-5932-5

Printed in the United States of America

The Other Side of the Game

Chapter I

ASHA

Why do black women have to embarrass themselves by showing the world how desperate they are, I thought as I watched the *Maury Povich Show.* Today's episode was about women who won't let go of their men no matter what they've done; and, of course, they picked the loudest, most ignorant sisters they could find. I watched a scruffy-looking deadbeat dad stroll out from backstage; then I thought that if the world ended tomorrow and aliens were to find tapes of *Jerry Springer, Ricki Lake* and all the other asinine programming offered on television, they would think that black women were a bunch of neck-swiveling, man-hungry idiots with low self-esteem. I'd rather die a tragic death than go around whining over some sorry-ass man. Life's too short for that shit.

All my life I've witnessed my mother and a host of cousins go through ridiculous, time-consuming, energy-draining mini-dramas with men not even worth speaking to in the first place. My father was one of them; he cheated on my mother in the seventies and then became a crackhead.

I guess, at seventeen, my mother was too young to be a very good judge of character but she would definitely live to regret her youthful folly when she was stuck with a one-year-old at eighteen. My parents were high school sweethearts, and my mother tried everything to make their relationship work but he could never meet her even halfway.

They're both dead now but they had an on-again, off-again relationship for many long, painful, age-inducing years.

She didn't learn anything from that mistake. A one-night stand with a cop who lived in the apartment upstairs produced my sister, Saundra. After their encounter, Phil Patterson took Mama out a few times. Maybe he would have married her if she had stopped trying to make things work with my father.

I remember having to stretch my quivering little arm around my mother's broad shoulders many times to comfort her after my dad disappointed us. Again.

I guess psychiatrists would say I have serious issues concerning relationships because of my childhood. I suppose they're right, but after all the stupid shit I've seen in my twenty-four years, they can kiss my ass.

When I was sixteen, I got pregnant by this guy named Dante. He had a high-top fade hairstyle with a blond streak across the front, new Air Jordans and a triple-fat goose coat to match every outfit. Dante was the best-looking and most popular boy in school. Even more important, he was from Uptown. At that time, Saundra and I were obsessed with people who lived in Harlem, the Bronx, Brooklyn, and Queens. We grew up in midtown Manhattan and because of that we were called Valley Girls. So to compensate for our shameful "white" locale, we imitated the cool kids who lived in the other boroughs. We wore huge gold doorknocker earrings and MC Lyte mushroom hairdos, which I now regret.

After getting gold fronts and purchasing a few oversize clocks to wear around our necks we were accepted into the much coveted "in" crowd, not necessarily because we were cool but because we looked damn good.

One night Saundra and I were at our friend T-Rock's house at the Butler projects in the South Bronx. Of course Mama didn't know we had traveled so far from midtown. We couldn't risk telling her because she might say "no" and *everybody* was going to be there. Besides, we had already bought matching black-and-white polka dot shirts from the Gap and Hammer pants just for this occasion and we weren't trying to hear "No."

We looked real good.

I'll never forget how excited we were the first time we rode the number 6 train into the Bronx. Saundra was grinning from ear to ear as the train screeched to a halt at the Tremont Avenue station. We ran down the stairs screaming "Yeah Boy!" and dancing the wop because we had managed to sneak off undetected by any of our mother's friends who we were sure would just happen to be riding the train that night. But neither of us wanted to admit our mutual terror as we walked through the playground over-crowded with hoodlums to get to T-Rock's building on the other side. They were some of the hardest-looking boys I had ever seen and Saundra didn't help quell my fear by pointing out that they were wearing colors owned by the notorious Decepticons street gang. I prayed their rival gang, the Autobots, wouldn't spray the block while we were there. After making it safely into the building, Saundra and I followed a herd of equally well-dressed teens up to the fifth floor.

The living room was crowded with sweaty drunk teenagers dancing to Big Daddy Kane's "Ain't No Half-Steppin" that was blasting from the speakers. It was so hot in there I remember being overly conscious of my hair after only two minutes inside. Saundra and I spent a long time trying to get my hair just right, and I wasn't trying to hear it napping up before Dante got a chance to appreciate it.

I knew he would be burning up the dance floor and that's just where he was. It was in style at the time for guys to battle in a cir-cle and impress everybody with really complex moves. Dante was double jointed so he could do things with his body that always got the crowd going "ooh" and "aah." I was all gassed up because I had the best-looking dancer there.

It wasn't long before Dante talked me into T-Rock's mother's bedroom and started running serious game. By the time he fin-ished complimenting me on my hair, my clothes and my face, I felt like the Queen of Sheba.

We had sex on top of T-Rock's mother's comforter with only

our bottoms off. While we were going at it, another couple wandered in with the same idea in mind and then backed out when they saw us. Later that night, I overheard Dante telling his boys that it was time to quit me now that he'd hit it.

A mixture of tears and eyeliner stung my eyes as I pushed my way through the stubborn crowd. The strobe light made it nearly impossible to detect Saundra amongst the mushroom-haired patch, not to mention the glimmering gold teeth reflecting like mirrors from oversize gold chains—but it was time to leave. *Now.*

Saundra was having a ball; only fourteen years old and high as a kite off St. Ides Malt liquor and doing a damn good running man dance with some guy wearing a twenty-inch high-top fade and leather bomber jacket. I tapped her on the shoulder and she shrugged me off thinking I was some hard-legged dude trying to cut in. The guy pointed behind Saundra to let her know I was there. She turned around and saw me with a face full of black tears and bloodshot eyes. She excused herself and we went home cursing Dante and everything Uptown.

A month later I realized I was pregnant when my very regular period failed to come. I cried so hard that night that I felt my body had become dehydrated.

Mama always tried to be supportive but I knew she would definitely be disappointed in me. I'd used to rather see my mother's angry face than her *I-wanted-more-for-you* look.

Before I told her, I had to call Dante.

His sister Keisha answered the phone and yelled for him to pick up the extension.

"Dante, it's Asha and we need to talk."

"What about?"

"I'm pregnant" I said slowly.

"OOOOH!" Keisha giggled.

"HANG UP THE FUCKING PHONE!" Dante screamed.

We heard another giggle and a discreet click.

"I can't help you." he said.

"So am I what am I going to do? You helped to make it."

"Sorry." *Click.*

It seemed like my life was over and every time I saw him at

school he would look the other way. To make matters worse, he told everyone what happened and everyone started staring at my stomach as if I would show so early.

I was the subject of a major scandal and the ridicule was tearing me apart. Saundra tried to defend me but the opposition was too great.

I finally told my mother one Saturday evening and after crying all night, we decided I'd have an abortion. That was during the month of September.

By the end of October, my problem had been solved. My baby was dead and a new Asha Mitchell was born. She wasn't taking no shit from *any* man.

The abortion and all of that other mess was eight years ago. Today, I make a decent living as an accessories buyer at the Herald Square location of Macy's department store, but I make an even better living as a serial dater. I have no intention of set-tling down or even being faithful to any one man. Right now I am a girlfriend to three different men: Brent, Nick, and Randall.

I live in a spacious one bedroom apartment on 14th Street and 6th Avenue in Manhattan. Nick, one of the rich guys I've been sleeping with for the past year, has promised to buy me a home on the beach so I'll be able to escape the city on weekends.

Since I live in one of Manhattan's more expensive areas and my building has a doorman, several women have asked me how I can afford the rent. But a question like that is not even worth an-swering. Any woman can find a man or men to pay her rent if she isn't dog-ugly or too lazy to do the work involved.

A sister with blue-black skin and trailing a waist-length blonde hair weave was hollering up in some brother's face on the *Maury Povich Show*, while the audience hooted, screamed, and egged the dumb duo on to even greater heights of public humiliation.

The sister squared off, shook the weave, and wagged her finger back and forth in the brother's face. "Hennessey is three years old and your sorry ass ain't nevah gave him a damned thang!" she screeched.

The sorry-looking deadbeat dad adjusted his do rag, hunched up his baggy pants and pushed her finger away. "You betta get up on outta mah face. How I know that baby's mine? You done gave it up to everybody roun' the way."

Maury Povich stepped in and suggested a DNA test.

If I had a hammer, I would use it to pulverize Maury Povich, the dark-skinned sister with the blonde weave, her dumb-ass man, and the poor little boy named Hennessey to save him from ever finding out that he was named after a bottle of liquor.

Chapter 2

SAUNDRA

Detective Phillip Patterson is my daddy and the sweetest man in the world. Before he left for work this morning he made me a delicious breakfast of hash browns, wheat toast, and a fruit salad. I feel so blessed to have someone in my life who loves me so much, and I can't imagine what I would do without him.

Mama had a stroke and died when I was sixteen. She was only thirty-five years old. I still can't understand why it took the paramedics so long to arrive. I dialed 911 as soon as mama crumpled to the floor.

The social worker said I could not stay with Asha because I was still underage. By that time, though, Daddy had bought a house in Queens and was living alone. We had always been close, so he took me in. We've had a wonderful life together over the past six years.

Around the time I moved in, Daddy met Evelyn Blake at a police officer's ball. She's a forty-something detective and just what my father needed. An intelligent, classy, sophisticated woman with a heart of gold. She also happens to be extremely well-groomed and attractive. And Evelyn wasn't only a treasure-find for Dad. If it wasn't for her, I wouldn't be who I am today. She introduced me to yoga, meditation techniques, and Taoism.

What no one can figure out is why Dad doesn't propose to Evelyn. In fact, she doesn't even live with us. Every time I raise the issue, Daddy rattles off a string of ridiculous excuses. Lately, I've stopped bringing up the subject. One day she'll wake up and realize that she deserves someone who is really into her enough to go the distance.

Since Evelyn came into my life, I have become a faithful student of Asian and African philosophy with an extensive library of books on both subjects. But what is more rewarding than merely reading the literature is its application. When I think of who I was before, I wince. My sphere of awareness was almost mechanical and I worshipped the major gods of this society: excuses, materialism, selfishness, and linear thought. These are deities I no longer wish to serve. Now I'm free of crippling limitations and I can concentrate fully on my goals. I'm a student at the Fashion Institute of Technology and I'll be graduating in May with a bachelor's degree in Fashion Design.

Finally, after four long years of hard work, I'll be able to open my own boutique. My father promised that as a graduation present he would get the ball rolling on renting me a little shop to sell my Afro-centric clothing at cost to poor women who can't afford the high prices charged elsewhere.

Asha graduated from the same college but she got only her associate's degree in Fashion Buying and Merchandising. It is unbelievable that Asha is an accessories buyer at Macy's department store with only a two-year degree. But I guess anything is possible when you'll throw your legs in the air to get a promotion. I think it's such a shame when a person bases their self-worth on the size of their behind and the roundness of their breasts.

I often wonder what will become of her when she no longer has a youthful body to flash around and she's forced to face whatever demon terrorizes her. It is pitiful that she hides her lack of self-confidence behind an ego so big it seems to be an entity unto itself.

But besides all that, I'm concerned about her physical well-being. No one likes to be made a fool of, and nowadays she's playing Russian roulette. She has a taste for expensive clothes and shoes that she can't afford, and she uses men to get them. I'm afraid that one day I'll get a call in the middle of the night saying that Asha was beaten up or killed by one of her conquests who decided to seek revenge.

I tell her my feelings because I feel that is my duty as a sister, but if she doesn't want to listen, all I can do is sit back and watch the chips fall. Besides, I have no time to argue with grown folks who are going to do what they want, anyway.

After working all day in the knitting lab at school and what seemed like an endless subway ride to my house in Hollis, I couldn't wait to lie down and relax. On Saturdays, the express E train to Queens always takes so long to get to Parsons Boulevard and Archer Avenue because it makes local stops on weekends.

As I walked down the block, I noticed my fiancé's lime green Hyundai parked in front. Yero and I have been close ever since I moved to this neighborhood in the eleventh grade. He is two years older than me and still lives around the corner with his mother and brother. He is honest, caring, and helpful.

Asha looks down on Yero because he only has a high school diploma and works at the post office. But having a man who is loving, balanced, responsible, intellectual and morally strong is more important than having a man who has money.

When I went in the house, I walked up the stairs and knocked on my father's door to let him know I was home.

"Come in," he answered loudly over his television.

"Hi, Dad, what's up?"

"Nothing much, just doing my afternoon workout. I guess you know your sidekick is here?"

"Yeah, I saw his car. Can I borrow twenty dollars? I need to go to Petland to get food for Blinky."

"Borrow? You don't have a job to pay it back." He laughed, getting up from his workout bench. I realized as he reached in his coat pocket for the money that his chest looked awfully pumped up.

"Dad, you're not on steroids, are you?"

"Of course not. I just been putting in some extra hours at the gym and, besides, even if I wanted to take steroids, it wouldn't be worth hearing your mouth."

I stuck my tongue out at him, grabbed the twenty out of his hand and shut the door.

Walking back down the stairs towards my room, I smelled my cinnamon incense burning. I can't afford to burn it all the time. That costs way too much money. I went in and found Yero reclining on my wood futon watching the Cartoon Network with Blinky, my three-foot yellow python wrapped around him.

"It took you long enough to get here. Me and Blinky missed you," he said with a fake pout.

I smiled and stepped over his long legs to extinguish the incense. "I missed you too, but before you get any more comfortable, we have to run over to Petland to get Blinky some nice juicy mice."

"Ah, the highlight of the day."

I walked over to my aquarium and sprinkled some chips into the water. Stooping down I watched my school of tropical fish swirl towards the surface and made sure everyone got a fair share. I looked at Yero and caught him staring at me. As he sat there, I noticed how wonderful he looked sitting in front of my black-and-white collage of tribesmen. His strong African features and thick locks had the same commanding majesty of the warriors, and his expression had the same pride and contentment as the sisters.

I sat down next to him and gave him a big hug.

"What was that for?"

"Just for being you." I mushed him playfully and smiled. He looked at me with those deep sleepy eyes of his.

"Why are you looking at me like that?" I asked, putting my hand on my hip in a fake sistah-girl fashion.

He touched underneath my chin gently and pulled my face towards his. When he kissed me, it was light and tender, without a hint of pressure. Actually, it felt like an embrace from a supernatural being and I was in a trance. If it wasn't for Blinky slithering impatiently off his body, we probably would have never stopped.

After our lips separated and we sat there examining each other with love-filled eyes, I stroked his dark brown face and was unable to speak. But that was all right, the silence said what I could not.

Chapter 3

ASHA

I slipped into a cobalt blue pencil skirt and a Rochas collarless floral brocade jacket in pale blue with aqua accents. It was a new outfit from a wonderful store called Bagutta. I slid my feet into a pair of silver Jimmy Choos as Brent frowned from his lounging position on the king-size bed that we had rocked and rolled on for most of the day. Brent was sitting up with his back against the plush headboard, in a beige Armani suit and matching shoes that were polished so hard, they seemed to gleam and reflect back every light in our luxurious hotel suite. His hands were folded neatly in his lap.

"It has taken you one full hour to bathe and get dressed. You still haven't done your hair or makeup."

"You're a handsome, refined gentleman, Brent. Don't you care what the woman on your arm looks like?"

"Yes, but I don't want to grow old waiting for her to get it together."

I ran my hands slowly up and down the sides of the skirt. "Why don't we forget about having a night on the town and just go back to bed?"

Brent sighed. "Asha, please stop fooling around. We're going to be late."

What a priggish fucking fuddy-duddy! If I'd said that to Nick or

Randall, my clothes would have been off my body and scattered all over the plush purple carpet within a matter of seconds. How on earth did this man's wife put up with him? What was her name? Amanda? She was probably glad that his boring ass wasn't home.

Time for makeup. I get such a kick out of staring at myself in a full-length mirror and admiring my knockout figure. My body is nothing short of perfection. The essence of womanhood itself. Flawless creamy skin with a slight red undertone gives it a warm subtle heat and a sexy glow that most women imitate with tacky bronzing powders. My Siamese-shaped eyes are hazel in color and sexy as all get out. And, although I'm only 5 feet 2 inches tall, I have the best pair of legs God ever created, and they look their best when they're freshly shaved and given the smooth sheen of sheer panty hose.

Once my makeup was on and my hair combed smoothly into a flip, I stood back to admire myself. Boy, I'm one great package and it is so no wonder that every man who isn't gay or retarded wants to be with me.

"Asha!"

I stopped preening. "Okay! Okay! Could you get my coat?"

We pulled away from the Parker Meridien hotel in his ivory pearl Infiniti G35 coupe.

"Where is this place?" he asked. Translation: Please tell me that you haven't picked a nightclub that Amanda might walk into.

"Relax, this place has been described as the temple of hip and it has the flash and brash to prove it."

A woman married to Brent Washington probably preferred dinner and a movie over rump shaking.

"What's the name of it?"

"Pergola 289. It's on Eleventh Avenue."

He turned west. "What do you like most about Pergola 289?"

"Stargazing."

"What?"

"The last time I was there, Wesley Snipes, Snoop Dog, and Terrence Dashon Howard were all in the house."

"Weren't there any female stars?" he asked dryly.

"I heard someone say that Vivica Fox was around."

Brent once said that it was safer to drive with both hands on the steering wheel. So, while he drove like he was trying to earn a fucking Boy Scout medal, I just stared out the window knowing that he wouldn't risk an accident by putting an arm around my shoulder.

I daydreamed about Nick Seabrook while Brent chattered on about the day-to-day problems at his job, how annoying Amanda was becoming, and what a joy it was to spend two nights in my presence.

Brent is an executive at Tiffany's jewelry store. He is married to a white lawyer. They have plenty of money but no kids because his wife has a fertility problem and doesn't like the idea of adoption. I get the impression that he doesn't have much of a social life, because he is always telling me that I "really know how to have a good time."

Whatever.

Nick, on the other hand, was a true romantic. He couldn't drive without leaning over for a kiss, touching my thigh, or drawing me closer to him. He couldn't watch a movie with me without making out or at least holding my hand and, above all, he always noticed what I wore and commented on how good it looked.

Nick was also a freak. He was in Houston on a business trip and I couldn't wait until he returned to New York.

"Asha, are you listening to me?"

I smiled sweetly at the man who paid my monthly rent, phone, cable and utility bills. "Of course, baby. It's just that I get a little jealous when you talk about Amanda."

Brent took one hand off the steering wheel and patted me . . . on the shoulder like he was my brother or uncle. "Sorry, sweetheart."

Whatever.

The club was located in an abandoned factory just a stone's throw from the Hudson River.

"Look at this place," Brent complained as he searched for a parking space. "There is a meat packing plant on one side of it and a park full of whores and crackheads on the other. It is a mugger's delight. We'll be lucky to make it in and out in one piece."

I soothed him with a peck on the cheek. "Would I bring my Main Man to a place where he could get injured?" Main Man was our pet name for Brent's dick.

He loosened his tie and grinned. "Let's get jiggy, sweetheart."

Jiggy, I thought as we crossed the threshold. *Real jiggy.* I planned to dance until the sweat poured down my back.

Pergola 289 was designed to look like a turn-of-the-century bordello. The walls were covered in red velvet and the floors were brick. The bases of its round tables were ornate iron grillwork. Faux Spanish moss dripped down the sides of the bar, which was shaped like a naked woman. A chandelier provided the only light, which left most of the place in shadows. There were many curvy sofas covered in a red brocade fabric around the walls; and to complete the atmosphere of decadence, four barely clad, busty women swung from red velvet swings suspended from the ceiling. The majority of the crowd was expensively dressed black folk but there were some young whites and a sprinkling of Asians. Those patrons who weren't dancing to the blasting rhythm & blues were tongue kissing on one of the sofas.

Brent whispered into my ear. "This is what I like about you, Asha. You're so adventurous."

We grinned at each other and hit the bar. A cosmopolitan with Grey Goose vodka for me and a cappuccino martini for him. We drank without talking, just grooving to the excellent music that the DJ was spinning. After the second round of drinks, I put my arms around his waist and our lips met for a kiss. Then we moved in closer. Normally, Brent hated public displays of affection, but even his conservative ass understood that a nightclub didn't count.

I was pressed right up against him and his tongue was halfway down my throat when the bartender, a woman dressed as a whore to keep the bordello theme going, stopped us with a friendly tap on Brent's shoulder. "Take it to the sofas, honey. That's why we have them."

Hell, we'd been in bed all day. It was time to dance.

Chapter 4

PHIL

She stood in the doorway of her apartment, which must have contained a gazillion kids judging by the noise coming from behind her. It could not have been cleaned in weeks judging by the funk that wafted over her shoulder. She was wearing a super tight, hot pink vinyl miniskirt and a red-and-black tube top. Her ashy looking feet were shoved into a pair of dirty gold sandals. The outfit told me she was either blind or on drugs. The sunken cheeks, missing teeth and once pretty eyes gave me my answer.

"Are you Maria Gonzalez?" I asked.

"Yes."

"I'm Detective Phillip Patterson and this is my partner, Detective Hugo Montana. I'd like to ask you a few questions, please."

She responded in rapid-fire Spanish aimed at Hugo.

Hugo answered her through gritted teeth. "Miss Gonzalez, do you speak English?"

"Yes."

"Then I want you to stop being so mutherfuckin' rude to my partner and pay attention to what he is saying."

Hugo and I have been partners for many years and we've been through this scene many, many times. Black suspects talk to me like he isn't in the room and Hispanics talk to him in Spanish, which leaves me totally out of the loop.

I waited a beat and then continued. "Miss Gonzalez, do you know a young man called Beany Cruz?"

She shook her head to mean no.

It was a lie and a stupid one at that.

"That's strange. Because you and Beany were seen laughing and talking together in the park last night and then again at the liquor store."

"You got a picture of this guy?"

She was stalling for time.

Hugo flashed a photo of the now-dead Beany in front of her face.

"Yeah. I know him."

"Do you know who shot him?"

"No."

"Do you care who shot him?"

That bought a gap-toothed grin to her face. "No. Can I go now?"

I unsnapped my cuffs. "Yes. We're all going right down to the 103rd Precinct. You're under arrest for murder."

Her eyes grew huge with fear. "I didn't kill nobody."

I cuffed her hands behind her back while Hugo rattled off her right to remain silent and all that shit. We both knew she hadn't killed Beany but her brother certainly had and the only way to find out where he was hiding was to put the squeeze on his crack-head sister.

It didn't take long to get the truth out of Maria Gonzalez. She held up pretty well through the reading of her Miranda rights but when we got downtown and it was time for fingerprinting and picture taking, brotherly love flew right out the window. She gave us what we needed to catch the real killer.

When I got home that evening, it was good to find the driveway empty. Saundra's boyfriend, Yero, spends so much time at our place, he might as well just move on in. As I opened the door, I could hear the sound of some music that sounded like monks chanting coming from her room.

I knocked on her door. "Honey, I'm home."

Saundra opened the door and kissed me lightly on the cheek. "Hi, Daddy. Did you have a good day?"

"I'm a cop. There is no such thing as a good day at work."

It was an old joke between us that started six years ago when Saundra first moved in. Back then she used to be really sad all the time about her mother's death and I didn't like to tell her about the human misery that I encountered each day. So, I'd make up these stories that had happy endings. One night I was just too tired to come up with another *I saved/rushed a little boy to the hospital and he is going to be fine* story and just told her that there was no such thing in my business as a good day at work.

When Saundra first came to live with me, I studied her every word and gesture, looking for signs of her mother that I could stamp out immediately. With all respect to the dead, Lola Smith was a weak, indecisive, and chronically depressed female who spent far too much time waiting for Mr. Right to show up on her doorstep. Saundra is the only child I will ever have in this lifetime and I wanted her to be the complete opposite—strong, educated, independent, with clear-cut goals and money of her own. To be honest, I'd hoped she would win a scholarship to one of those fancy girls' schools like Spelman or Barnard and land one of those jobs where she'd have a big office and a six-figure paycheck. But she decided to study the rag trade and open a boutique. That's okay by me. Saundra has turned out to be a terrific young woman and there is nothing wrong with raising a family and selling clothes. I'm going to give her the start-up money and pay for her wedding to Yero. Then I'm going to sit her down, tell her a truth that has always needed telling and live the life that will make me happy.

Chapter 5

EVELYN

Phil is taking me to B.B. King's blues club in Manhattan so I'm trying to find the right pair of shoes to go with my lime green wrap dress and listen to my best friend, Josephine Styles, at the same time. That's what I like about Phil. I don't have to beg him to take me out or buy me a thoughtful gift. It was his idea for us to hang out in the city tonight and he even picked out this new dress for me to wear. He is a wonderful boyfriend. But just because he hasn't given me an engagement ring, I have to listen to Mama's mouth and Josephine's mouth. They harangue me constantly but I don't pass the stress on to Phil. He and I agreed that as soon as Saundra moved out of the house, it would be my time. Phil said that back in his hometown of Dayton, he saw many relationships fall apart simply because two grown women could not share the same space in peace. I agreed to wait for him to handle his business with his daughter. I'm happy with the way things are. So, that's that. Or it should be.

Josephine and Mama think that Phil is dragging his feet for some unknown reason and that I should push his back up against the wall and drag a wedding date out of him. That's crazy. I've waited six years and Saundra is getting married in a few months. Why should I start some mess now?

Even now, instead of helping me pick out the shoes, Josephine is sitting on the side of my bed, running her mouth, "Sweetie, when is his daughter getting married?"

I waved my hand airily, trying to look unconcerned. "In June."

"So, why can't Phil buy your engagement ring now?"

"We're both always so busy. The subject just hasn't come up."

Her voice rose. "Hasn't come up?"

I shushed her. "Keep your voice down. Mama is trying to get some sleep."

Josephine lives down the street with her husband and two handsome teenaged sons. I love her but right now she was creating negative energy.

"I'm surprised your mother can sleep at all with her only child dangling on a hook for the past six years." Josephine slipped off her shoes and put her feet up on the ottoman.

"Why should I rush this man down the aisle, Josephine? I've never been interested in having children. I'm not feeling insecure because I always know where he is, and we're only going to City Hall when we *do* tie the knot. We can just jump up and do that any time."

Josephine was still a brainwashed sistah. Meaning that her hair was streaked with a red that is unnatural to African-American women and it was also chemically relaxed. She flipped it over one shoulder now. "Fine. Call him now and tell him to jump up and marry you next Friday. I'll go with you."

"Phil is one of the last good men left and I don't plan to lose him by listening to you," I said.

"Don't get me wrong, Evelyn. I like Phil and everything, but something just isn't right. I think he must be one of those commitment-phobic men who I read about in this book called *Men Who Can't Love.*"

"Phil definitely loves me!" I protested.

She took a long swig of Sunny Delight. "Yes, he loves you, but the idea of saying "I do" probably makes him wake up screaming in fear. I'm not putting him down. It's a serious emotional condition and he'll need to see a shrink to get over it."

"How can you drink that stuff? Why not just buy orange juice?"

"Don't change the subject."

"Actually, I am going to change the subject."

"Fine. Just ask Phil to set a date and see what he says."

"I don't want him to feel pressured."

"Pressured? After six years? Puh-leeze, girl. He's lucky you haven't shot his ass."

"Josephine, I've been married before and it flopped. Plus, it's not like I don't have any life outside of Phil."

"Something just doesn't seem right to me, Evelyn."

I'd had enough. "How are your boys?"

She sighed. "You just saw them yesterday. They're fine."

"Look, Josephine. I believe in Phil and you're just going to have to respect that."

She clicked the remote and started surfing for something enlightening to watch. "Fine. I'll never bring it up again."

"Good."

Josephine and Mama need to handle the procrastinators in their own lives. Mama and the local butcher have been flirting with each other for the past ten years. She spends hours standing in that store talking to him about God knows what and sometimes he comes to our house and they yammer some more. Has he ever taken her to the theater, out to a nice romantic dinner or held hands and traded kisses with her during a movie? No. Does he buy her a card and a gift on her birthday? No. Does he show up with candy and flowers on Valentine's Day? No. So, what is she pushing me for? The butcher has it made. Mama listens to and counsels him about all his personal problems. They cheer each other on. Talk about their disappointments and sharing what few dreams they each have left. In other words, he has a free girlfriend without any of the responsibility (financial or sexual) that goes along with a real romantic relationship.

And Josephine? She and I have plans to quit the police force and open up a weekend spiritual retreat for women in upstate New York. But every time we get ready to file for incorporation and move forward, her husband convinces her to wait. I listen to her complain endlessly about how tired she is of him holding us back. Then she'll stiffen her backbone and promise me that

we're really going to do it. Next month. He drags around looking
sad for a few days and when that doesn't work, he becomes mean
and starts nitpicking at everything she does until her migraines
start up again. This has been going on for over a year. I'm beginning to think that I should just start the retreat by myself but
Josephine and I have been friends since high school and I don't
want to alienate her.

Today I wrote an advertisement for what should be our first
program:

> *Real Life Retreat Center, Irvington, New York*
> *Ever feel like you aren't living for yourself? Just going along
> with someone else's program? Living by someone else's standards?
> Traveling on someone else's schedule? It isn't too late to turn your
> life around. Wake up! Take a few baby steps toward living the life
> you want to have. During this weekend, we will unpack some of
> your old dreams and look at what you'd really like to do with your
> life. We will visualize a happier life for you and explore ways for
> you to get it. It's not too late if you start right now. Cost: $495.*

Mama can't get the butcher to commit to simply being her
boyfriend. Josephine can't get her husband to leave her alone
long enough for us to find out if our idea has merit. Why should
I listen to either one of them and start nagging Phil about a wedding date?

Chapter 6

SAUNDRA

Medical studies have proved that vegans are up to 40 percent less likely to die of cancer and 30 percent less likely to get heart disease. We are also less prone to high blood pressure and diabetes. This is one reason why Yero, Evelyn, and I don't eat flesh. The other reason is that veganism is not just a diet but an attitude of reverence for the sanctity of life. It is a spiritual appreciation and acknowledgement of all God's creatures.

So the three of us are having veggie burgers and vegan pizza for dinner.

I was chopping up the green peppers, celery, pecans and parsley. Yero was mashing the chickpeas and Evelyn was spreading the vegan pizza dough when Daddy walked in with his friend, Hugo.

Hugo Montana is a Latino officer who has been Daddy's best friend for as long as I could remember.

The two big detectives greeted us cheerfully and then unpacked a box of Popeye's fried chicken and a tub of mashed potatoes covered with gravy. Dad grabbed two beers from the refrigerator and they tore into the meal like they'd never eaten before.

Evelyn, who was wearing a gorgeous yellow caftan and matching headwrap, had been singing as she prepared the pizza. Now she was quiet and a frown creased her forehead.

"Don't worry, Evelyn," I said loudly. "Daddy is beginning to see the error of his ways. He won't be eating that junk much longer. The other day I caught him drinking some of my soy milk."

"I had already poured my coffee," Daddy replied. "There was no other milk in the house."

Hugo munched a drumstick. "Leave us in peace, *chica*. We've just had a rough eight hours. First, we had to arrest a woman just so she'd tell us where her murdering brother was hiding, but then when we got to the address she gave us, he was already on a plane to the Dominican Republic. Now we'll have to do a whole bunch of paperwork to get him back to the United States. What makes it so bad is that both he and Beany Cruz put together ain't worth the price of a postage stamp.

"Who is Beany Cruz?" asked Yero.

"The dead guy." Hugo shrugged. "Some penny ante crack dealer."

"That was just this morning's work," groused Phil.

Hugo nodded. "After that, we get another call. This guy beat his grandmother to death with a candlestick holder. He gets down to the precinct and starts playing like he's crazy. Only we know he ain't crazy. Then, when that didn't work, he tells us he didn't do it. That he has a violent twin brother who hated the old lady. So we go back to the block and talk to the neighbors again. They look at us like we been smokin' angel dust or something. Then we get it. There ain't no twin brother. In fact, there ain't no other family around at all. So then your daddy got mad and when we got back down to the station, I had to keep him from killing that fool."

Yero had stopped mashing the chickpeas. He loves cop stories. "Then what happened?"

"We booked the fool and threw him in jail."

Daddy grinned at Yero. "Why don't you take the officer's exam, man? Quit fooling around. You know that's what you really want to do."

"No, he doesn't," Evelyn said. "It's just like in the old days when the lives of proper ladies were very structured and stultifying; they were always willing to listen to stories of what they called fallen women. Of course, they pretended to shake their heads in disgust, but the tales really added some color to their dreary lives."

Yero pretended to be hurt. "What are you saying? That my life is dreary?"

Evelyn laughed and patted him on the back. "Of course not, honey. I just meant that you sell stamps all day and uh . . ."

I laughed. "Evelyn, why don't you quit while you're ahead."

Yero went back to mashing the chickpeas as we all chuckled.

Hugo pointed a fork in my direction. "So, *chica*, I hear you're going to be a bride. Is that true?"

Evelyn answered for me. "Saundra is going to be the most gorgeous bride in the history of brides. I've been waiting for this wedding for a long time."

She and daddy locked eyes and I could feel the negative energy.

I hurried to cover the silence. "Are you coming to my wedding, Hugo?"

"If I'm invited."

"Of course you're invited. Don't be silly."

"Can I have the first dance?"

"No, my first dance will be with Yero."

He continued to tease me. "What about the second dance?"

"Sorry. That one belongs to Daddy."

Hugo sighed and took a long swig of beer.

"This wedding is going to cost me a pretty penny," Daddy said. "Have you two found a church yet?"

"We're getting married in Central Park," answered Yero. "Churches make some people feel uncomfortable. We have friends who believe in a higher power but it isn't always a Christian God."

Daddy was about to say something but Evelyn gave him a *leave the kids alone* stare.

"What about the party? Where is that going to be?"

"Daddy, we found one place over near Jamaica Estates. It's called The Crystal Palace. It is really beautiful but they want too much money, so we're still searching."

Hugo shrugged. "How much?"

"Two hundred fifty dollars per person."

"*Ay, Dios mio!*"

Daddy went to the refrigerator and got another beer. "Humph! Oh, my God in Spanish isn't enough. You need to say it in Italian, German, Hungarian and Yiddish. Two hundred fifty dollars per person! Are they crazy? Does that include an open bar all night with premium brand liquor? What type of food do they serve for that kind of money?"

Yero cleared his throat. "Phil, we're not planning to serve any alcoholic beverages at the reception."

"I'm expected to shell out two hundred fifty dollars per person and sit there stone cold sober?"

"Get a grip, Phil," said Evelyn. "Saundra has already said that it is too expensive and they're looking at other places."

"Yeah, Daddy. Calm down."

Evelyn added coarse salt and Roma tomatoes to the vegan pizza dough. She looked very unhappy and I couldn't help feeling sorry for her. We should all be planning her wedding to Daddy. She still lived with her mother on Long Island. Daddy lived in a three-bedroom house with me in Queens. The two of them must have had sex at hotels because she was never in his bed here and this whole silly mess had been going on for six years.

What on earth was she getting out of the relationship? Why didn't she just end it?

How could Daddy be so wonderful with one female (me) and so self-centered and callous with another (Evelyn)?

I combined the chickpeas, pecans, bread crumbs, carrots, pepper, celery and parsley in a big bowl.

Yero and I dug our hands into the mixture, smiled at each other and started making patties.

Chapter 7

ASHA

Nick Seabrook was in town!
He called me at work and asked me out to dinner, but I had a far more exciting idea. I was going to drive him crazy.

Nick was the gorgeous twenty-six-years-young playboy heir to a chain of soul food restaurants that his parents built from scratch. Seabrook's Soul Food had an outlet in every major city except New York. He had an MBA from the Wharton School of Business and spent most of his time traveling cross-country checking up on the managers who were in charge of the day-to-day operations of each establishment. I had no idea why Nick kept a condominium in New York since he usually stayed with me. Every time I asked him, he said that he wants to marry me someday and we'll live there. I know he is only teasing about that, but it doesn't matter. I'm not marrying anybody. Ever. I love my life just the way it is.

There is a four-star Italian restaurant about three blocks away from my apartment. Normally, they don't offer take-out service but I spend so much money there, I was able to convince the owner that sending a feast for two up to my place was good for future business.

Once my dining room table (which seats eight) was set with

fine white linen, heavy silverware, delicate china, Waterford crystal glasses, and two red candles, it was time for me to get dressed.

By the time I opened the door to let him in, I was wearing a waist-length, shiny black wig with a center part, false eyelashes, red lipstick, a red miniskirt with no panties on underneath, red stiletto heels, and my only top was a red silk, see-through bra.

Nick's lips parted in a great big smile and seeing the sexy gap between his two front teeth made me want to hit my knees and blow him right then and there. But that would have spoiled my plan.

His eyes rested on my nipples and a "Wow!" escaped his juicy lips.

He reached out to grab me but I wriggled away and gave him a chaste kiss on one cheek. "Nick! How delightful to see you. Please hang up your coat and make yourself comfortable. Dinner will be ready in a moment."

It was hard for me to keep a straight face as I marched demurely toward the kitchen like a housewife in a 1950s television show.

I was pulling the heated veal parmigiana from the stove when Nick came up behind me. His erection pressed against my ass and made me shiver. I almost dropped the veal. One strong arm held me by the waist while he used his other hand to go up under the tiny skirt.

"Forget the food, baby," he whispered into my ear.

I slapped his hands and arms away. "Nick. I've got a four-course meal here and I'd really appreciate it if we could enjoy the food while catching up on each other's lives."

"Why is it so quiet in here?" Normally my place is alive with music.

"I didn't want any noise to interfere with our elegant dinner conversation."

He took a step back and smiled. "What kind of game are you playing, Asha?"

I handed him a platter of calamari and tried to look innocent. "Why, whatever do you mean, Nick? I am a lady having a gentleman over for dinner. Now, would you please help me out here?"

"Baby, if you want me to sit through a four-course meal, you're going to have to change that outfit."

I ignored the suggestion and tried not to giggle.

Pour the water. Fill the wineglasses. Load up our plates with calamari and antipasto. Sit down and take a bite.

He watched every move I made with a hunger in his eyes that made me yearn for him like I never had before. My fork clicked back and forth against the plate. He didn't move. He didn't say a word.

"Aren't you going to eat, honey? It really is delicious."

"Okay, Asha. I'll play along."

"So, how is the restaurant business?"

Nick swallowed one piece of calamari. "Business is booming, Asha. Now, I've finished my appetizer. What's the next course?"

He didn't even chew it! I had planned to march him through the appetizer, then some bread and cheese with the veal as the third course and me as the fourth. But if he was going to throw whole chunks of food down his throat, we'd end up in St. Vincent's hospital's emergency room instead of my big round bed.

"It's a delicious new bread and there are three different kinds of cheese."

We had been sitting at opposite ends of the long table. Now, he picked up his plate and came over to sit beside me.

"I've missed you, Asha."

"How sweet!"

He started to say something else and then stopped.

"Nick, you're always doing that. Please say whatever it was that you started to say."

He cleared his throat. "There is something but it has to wait for the right day and the right time."

"Why? Are you getting married or something? You can tell me, I won't get mad."

He looked at me with a very queer expression on his face. "I know you won't."

"Well, are you?"

"What?"

"Getting married?"

"No, I'm not. Let's change the subject, okay?"

For some strange reason, I felt better knowing that Nick wasn't getting ready to tie the knot. "Okay. What do you want to talk about?"

"I brought you something."

"What?"

"A present."

Music to my ears. The last present Nick bought me was a silver STS V8 Cadillac with a Bose 5.1 studio surround sound system. I kept it in a garage on 45th Street.

"Where is it?"

"In my coat pocket."

"That's nice," I replied coolly. "It can wait until after dessert."

He groaned and placed a hand on my thigh. "Asha, please. Stop it." There were beads of sweat on his forehead

"Oh, all right. We can skip the bread and cheese."

Nick paused for a moment, gave me a wicked grin and left the room. When he came back, there was a long slender box in his hand.

He placed it in front of my plate but didn't sit back down.

As I ripped off the heavy pink wrapping, he started to strip. By the time I lifted my new diamond necklace from the silk-lined box, Nick's shirt had dropped to the floor and his belt was unbuckled. I couldn't take my own game anymore.

The heat in the room suddenly reached a thousand degrees and I was on my knees unzipping his pants before he had time to make another move.

Chapter 8

SAUNDRA

Most shampoos contain sodium lauryl sulfate, a chemical that has cancer causing properties. That is why I use honeysuckle rose shampoo. It doesn't create any kind of lather or suds but at least it doesn't endanger my health.

With my hair still wet I sat on the floor in my room for Evelyn to towel it dry and oil my locks.

"We need to order invitations and put together a guest list," Evelyn said. She made this announcement right out of the blue as though we had been having a discussion about my wedding. We'd known each other long enough for me to understand that she had been busy in a spirited interior monologue while I was in the shower.

Yero and Evelyn both came from huge families while I only had Asha and a few friends. "Would you like to invite your kinfolk?" I asked.

"Just my mother if you don't mind, sweetheart."

"Of course I don't."

I knew that what Evelyn really wanted was an invitation to help me with every detail of my upcoming nuptials, but it was something I really wanted to do with Asha and I didn't know how to say so without hurting her feelings. So I just quietly looked at the dozens of blown-up pictures that covered my walls. Mama was in every single one of them.

"Sweetheart, are you sure you don't want to get in touch with them?"

Them. Mama's family. The clan who had turned their collective backs on Mama long ago because she refused to give up on Asha's drug addicted father. The clan who had come to her funeral, offered me and Asha a home, and then dismissed us when I decided to move in with my own father and Asha decided to keep our old apartment to remain independent.

"No. Something might go wrong. It is supposed to be the happiest day of my life and I won't let anyone take that away from me."

Evelyn stood up for a moment to adjust the chair she was sitting in. "How about an engagement party? We could have them all over for a two-hour affair so they can meet Yero. Any issues that come up would be dealt with there, and then everyone would be calm on your wedding day."

"Evelyn, it's not like Asha and I were accustomed to being around them when Mama was alive. It would be more of a getting-to-know-each-other gathering than an actual reunion."

"So, what's wrong with that?" Evelyn asked calmly.

Evelyn started parting my locks in small sections, oiling the scalp as she went. "I just don't have the energy."

"If everything goes well then the children you have with Yero will have a nice extended family to love them. Children can never get enough love."

"I'm sorry, Evelyn, but if Mama was alive, she wouldn't go running after them. I don't want to either and Asha will hit the ceiling if I even suggest it."

"Asha lives in fear of everything. Commitment. Forgiveness. True intimacy. I taught you better than that."

I said nothing.

Evelyn sighed. "Okay, sweetheart. I respect your decision."

I searched my mind for something other than the wedding to discuss. "My graduation ceremony is going to be held at Madison Square Garden."

"Oh, how wonderful! This is a year of many blessings for you, and I can't think of anyone who deserves it more."

That's what I liked about Evelyn. In spite of the fact that I'd nixed her idea of a Smith family reunion, she didn't pout or press the issue. She always just wanted me to be happy.

Evelyn massaged the oil into my scalp and patted the top of my head. "I'm finished. Would you like to go shoe shopping with me?"

At any other time I would have grabbed my coat and joined her but the conversation about Mama's family had made me a little sad. It was time to meditate. I needed to get silent inside so that my true inner voice could guide me.

Chapter 9

ASHA

Saundra is my heart but one of these days I'm going to tie her down, put some makeup on her face and do something with that hair. After that, I'll shake her by the shoulders until her survival instinct kicks in and she decides to become the next Vera Wang. Imagine working four years for a fashion design degree and then using it to create clothes for people who can't pay for them. What kind of sense does that make? She'll end up a poverty-stricken old woman, tottering around on a cane with that dull-ass Yero at her side and nothing to show for almost fifty years of labor.

That won't happen to me. I will not end up as an elderly, destitute black woman.

To make sure that I never catch the fatal "money doesn't matter, happiness is what is truly important in life" disease, I generally avoid people (with the exception of Saundra because she is my sister) who already have it. In fact, Randall is the only man I sleep with who is poor but he makes up for that between the sheets. Big time.

Randall is a twenty-eight-year-old accountant who toils away in the back room at some two-bit firm in Brooklyn. I met him about six months ago at B Smith's, a playground for black professional men and women. He was dressed in a beautiful suit that he later confessed he'd been saving money for almost a year. He sat down on the stool next to me and we silently appraised each other. After an average "getting to know you" conversation, we exchanged numbers and the rest is history.

Since then, he has maxed out his credit cards: there's been a weekend in the Bahamas, exotic restaurants, orchids, Godiva chocolates and cellar wines. CHA-CHING!

Tonight we're staying in to watch the *Godfather* trilogy. I prepared turkey sandwiches, popcorn, and a couple of cold beers. I hope he wasn't expecting a four-course meal because I don't cook for any man. They get way too comfortable with that shit. He will be eating Lunchables while he's dating me unless *he* decides to play Martha Stewart.

The hour is approaching eight and he should be here momentarily. I went to the bathroom and I realized my hair was a little frizzy, so I wet it a little to get my curls happening again.

After I channel surfed for twenty minutes, my doorman announced Randy's arrival.

"Hi, hon," I said, kissing him sweetly on the cheek.

"You're in a great mood this evening," he said playfully, while walking into the kitchen. "Did something exciting happen at work?"

My eyes were on the big gold box he placed gently down on the table.

"Huh," he insisted, expecting an answer.

"What did you say?"

"Never mind. I bought something for you."

I suppressed the desire to jump up and down and clap with excitement. Grinning, he motioned for me to join him as he opened the box. I stood over it with pop eyes as he slowly lifted the lid. To my horror, a tiny brown puppy was asleep at the bottom of the box wearing a big red bow around his silky neck. That's when I noticed the holes on the side of the box.

"He's adorable; what kind of dog is he?" I asked, managing a fake squeal of excitement as I scooped the drowsy pooch gently into my arms.

"A golden retriever. I knew you'd like him. I always think about you being alone in here and I decided to do something about it."

Was this supposed to be a guard dog? What an idiot!

As Randy turned to sit down on the sofa, I briefly pictured him *and* the dog going back into the elevator and far away from me. But what the hell, he's a good listener, enjoys sex, and is trying to get some more credit cards to keep me happy. I just hope all his future tokens of affection will be inanimate.

I took a deep breath and carried my new roommate into the next room.

Chapter 10

SAUNDRA

Daddy was upset when I told him about Evelyn's idea. It was a quiet weekday evening and we were watching the big screen TV downstairs in the living room. A commercial that was hawking ridiculously expensive sneakers interrupted a program on the mystery of Stonehenge when I told him about the proposed engagement party.

He had been reclining in the La-Z-Boy. Now, he snapped the clutch and the chair sprung upright. He frowned at me sitting cross-legged on our plush beige carpet. "Here, in this house?"

"Well, Daddy, it wouldn't make sense to rent space. We're already going to shell out money for a reception hall. Besides, I think getting together in an intimate setting is the whole point."

"Do you realize what a difficult position that would put me in?"

"What do you mean?"

"Nothing," he muttered.

I sensed that I was onto something. "Tell me, Daddy."

He stroked his chin and didn't answer.

"Daddy?"

"No one in Lola Smith's family has ever laid eyes on me. What could I possibly say to them after all this time?"

"They saw you at the funeral."

"Oh, yeah. Right." He lapsed into silence again.

I was afraid to ask the next question but the energy in the room had become real weird. Why?

"Does mama's family dislike you for some reason?"

"Probably."

"Talk to me, Daddy!"

"About what?"

Now he was going to play dumb.

"What they might be holding against you."

Daddy exhaled noisily. "Saundra, when your mother got pregnant with you, she expected me to marry her. She told me that. She also told her sisters that we were going to tie the knot. I'm guessing that when it didn't happen, she was very embarrassed. I'm also guessing that they hate me for being another guy who let her down."

"This isn't like you, Daddy."

"What do you mean?"

"It isn't like you to put your own interests before mine. I mean, this engagement party is about me and Yero and the children we're going to have. It's not about you or your discomfort. I'm very disappointed in you right now."

He looked like I had slapped him. "Aw, baby, I'm sorry. You're right. I'm being selfish."

"Daddy, can I ask you something?"

Now he looked wary. "Yes, but I'm not promising to answer."

"Fair enough."

"Okay, then."

"Are you ever going to marry Evelyn?"

He looked relieved that it wasn't another question about Mama or her family. "No, Saundra."

"Why not?"

"It's a long story."

I was truly bewildered. "A long story? But you two are still together. If she has done wrong, why are you still in the relationship?"

Daddy closed his eyes, then opened them. "I'll tell you all about it someday, but not before you graduate and get married."

He held up a hand for me to be quiet and then kept on talking.

"Just for the record, the only thing Evelyn has ever done wrong is to bring up the idea of getting your mother's family together in this house."

Not knowing what else to do, I stared at the television screen like it held the answer to the Dead Sea Scrolls.

"How do you think Asha would feel at a party like that? I mean, at least you had me to take care of all your needs. The poor girl worked two fast food jobs to keep that dinky apartment together. Lola's people wouldn't help her at all. If I hadn't sent her money, she would have suffered even more. Asha probably doesn't want to mix with them any more than I do."

"Forget it, Daddy."

"Asha has always had it harder than you. I used to tell Lola that she leaned on Asha too much . . . always confiding in that girl about her troubles . . . it isn't right to burden a young person with adult problems that they don't know how to solve."

I had always known that Mama shared her problems with Asha. Maybe because Asha was the spitting image of her. Maybe because Asha was the eldest. No one would ever really know why and the conversation was beginning to depress me in a real big way.

"Let's watch the show, Daddy."

He patted my shoulder and sighed loudly. "I'd walk on hot coals for you, Saundra. If you want a family reunion here, just name the date. All right?"

My words inched their way out through gritted teeth. "I said, forget it."

Chapter II

PHIL

As soon as Saundra spat out the words "forget it" for the second time, I climbed out of the Laz-E-Boy, went over to the wet bar, which I'd installed right after buying the house, and poured half a glass of whiskey; I drank it straight down.

"Don't you want to know why I never married Lola?"

"I already know the answer to that, Daddy."

"You do?" I struggled to look straight at Saundra but my eyes just wouldn't focus on that section of the room. They grew so wide with fear that it seemed I could actually see everything in the house from the finished basement to the socks upstairs in my underwear drawer. I poured another cup of courage and drank it before daring to look toward Saundra again. Her face seemed blurry and indistinct. I couldn't determine whether she looked angry or triumphant. I had known this day would come but it wasn't supposed to be like this—the revelation was to have been mine to control. How was I supposed to explain the years of dishonesty?

The liquor was making the heat from my sweatsuit unbearable. My sweat socks felt like snug ninety-degree heaters. I strained to see her body language through the whiskey haze. She didn't seem tense at all. In fact, her wrist moved languidly as she clicked the remote control, surfing for another program. I opened my mouth to tell her the history behind my lies but something, perhaps the instinct of a cop, told me to just keep my mouth shut for just one more second.

It was regrettable, I thought, that Lola had up and died just as I was beginning to live. It was also a shame that I came from a long line of men who did not walk away from their children. If I had been able to let go of Saundra, she wouldn't be suffering through what must be unimaginable pain right now. I watched her stare at the television screen as though our relationship had not just changed forever. That was Patterson blood at work. Lola would have been crying, cursing, scratching my face and threatening to shoot me with my own gun. She had never been able to look disappointment in the eye, square her shoulders and soldier on as her daughter was doing right now. Lola had had a bad habit of taking on people and projects that any sane person would have run away from. Then, when they didn't work out, she was not able to take responsibility for her poor choices. Oh, no! She would whine about being born under an unlucky star, cursed by fate and other endless nonsense that simply drove me crazy. Then, when that crisis had passed, Lola would go find another stupid-ass situation to get involved in and the wheel started to turn all over again.

I was proud of Saundra. So proud that I put the cap back on the whiskey bottle, screwed it on tight and placed it back in the cabinet. Then, with a smile so wide that every tooth in my mouth was showing, I crossed the room and grabbed both of Saundra's hands. I kissed her once on each cheek. "I should have known that you, of all people, would be in my corner. Thank you, from the bottom of my heart."

Saundra patted my shoulder. "I've known for a long time why you didn't ask Mom to marry you, but don't worry, Daddy. There are plenty of things you can work on before you ruin things with Evelyn."

I blinked twice. "Honey, it isn't a disease. I can't just take a pill and make it go away."

She laughed softly. "Sure you can. Twenty years ago it was different, but now doctors know how to treat people who suffer from commitment phobia. The success rate is quite high."

I pressed the palm of my hand against my forehead, murmuring, "commitment phobia." I sank back down into the La-Z-Boy recliner, my shoulders slumped forward. My eyes found their way to the television but they didn't see a goddamned thing.

Chapter 12

EVELYN

It was early in the morning when Phil called to tell me off about encouraging Saundra to invite her mother's family over for an engagement party. I had strapped on my gun and checked to make sure I had handcuffs. Then I set my navy blue policewoman's cap just right on top of my locks when the phone rang. In the six years that Phil and I have known each other, we may have had two disagreements so his nasty attitude really caught me by surprise. I sat down on my bed and imagined that I was protected from his coldness by a warm yellow ball of light that was encircling my body. I imagined that the ball of light was impenetrable. That it couldn't be pierced by bullets, fists, or words. With the light protecting me, I was able to remain unafraid and, therefore, calm.

"Why couldn't you talk to me about this before mentioning it to Saundra?" he asked.

"You've never asked me to clear anything with you before talking to Saundra," I said.

"Didn't I tell you that Saundra is the product of a one-night stand? That I never really dated Lola Smith? That the so-called relationship we had was just Lola's imagination working overtime?"

"Yes."

"Then what could I possibly say to the Smith family? Tell me that, Evelyn."

The yellow light cracked a little because the first time I got married it was to a very nice boy of eighteen. We were the same age. I was pregnant. Dad had been dead eight years and Mama was working long hours as a nurses' aid. Jerry Turner and I loved each other, but while planning for the wedding, our families bickered so much that we just ran down to city hall and came back hitched. They had a fit! On top of that, it turned out that mine was a tubal pregnancy. I lost the embryo and almost died in the process.

"Phil, I just didn't want the kids to have any discord at their wedding."

"Well, just don't say any more about it."

"Okay."

"You're mad now, right?"

"No, Phil. I'm not angry. I seem to be keeping my mouth shut about a lot of things these days." Now where did that come from?

"What is that supposed to mean?"

There was silence between us and I had to come clean before it became just too uncomfortable.

"It means that I'd like to have an engagement ring, Phil."

His voice softened. "Look, sweetheart. Just let me march my daughter down the aisle first. Okay?"

I couldn't understand why I had to wait so long just to get a preliminary ring on my finger but the yellow light of protection had faded. I was vulnerable.

"Sure, Phil. Whatever you say."

Chapter 13

ASHA

Clinique Superdefense Triple Action Moisturizer SPF25 was the only scent on my skin as I slipped into a black leotard, matching jeans, and a pair of Prada loafers to prepare for my next hotel rendezvous with Brent. The only fancy item I planned to take was a black Dolce & Gabbana snakeskin bag with a zodiac buckle that Nick had bought for me.

"Meet me tonight at the Sherry Netherland," he had whispered into my phone at work.

We never met at the same hotel twice. The poor fool honestly believed that this would keep Amanda from finding out about his affair. Why hasn't someone told him just how resourceful a suspicious wife or girlfriend can be? Is he crazy? We can track a brother's movements like a bloodhound chasing an escaped slave. But I didn't care enough about Brent to share this basic fact with him. Besides, he is a forty-four-year-old man. If he doesn't understand women by now, nothing I do or say will help.

There was nothing out of the ordinary about his phone call but I still felt annoyed. It was getting harder and harder to spend time with Brent. He talked about the exact same things at the exact same moment every single time. I'd heard all his jokes and the punch lines weren't going to change. He got on my nerves but not enough for me to quit seeing him. My savings account was fatter than Biggie Smalls and steadily growing. It was my old age fund, so I wouldn't end up broke and ill like Mama. If I quit screwing Brent, then the rent, phone, electricity and cable bills would have to come out of my salary. There was no way I could ask Nick to pay them. He was already buying my clothes, shoes, and jewelry.

I didn't have the energy to find another married man to pay all my basic bills, and single guys always threw it up in your face when you didn't do something they asked for. Married men went along with anything that would keep you from asking them to leave their wives.

So, I would screw him, grab this month's check and be home in time to watch Jay Leno, but dressing up for the occasion was simply out this time. I just couldn't summon up that much enthusiasm.

I drove my own car to the assignation so he wouldn't have to drop me off afterwards. That would have meant making even more conversation with him.

What the hell was wrong with me lately?

Probably too much Nick Seabrook. Spending time with him always made it hard for me to enjoy the company of other men. This, of course, is exactly what happens to all women. A man gets under their skin and they stop handling their business.

This type of behavior had to end.

I put a big smile on my face and sailed through the hotel lobby like I had just arrived on the Concorde to have a tryst with P. Diddy.

He greeted me at the door with a dozen red roses and a bottle of Cristal.

"You've been on my mind all day," he said when we were naked under the covers and swilling champagne.

"Ooh, Brent, after you called, it was hard for me to concentrate on anything else, either."

He smiled. "Baby, if Amanda was more like you, I wouldn't be here."

I kissed him hard on the lips to postpone the upcoming Amanda monologue.

"You're a hard act to top, Asha. Do you know that?"

I ran my fingers lightly up and down the inside of his thigh.

"Asha, I can't get enough of you," he whispered.

"How much of me do you want tonight?" I murmured back.

Brent answered by pouring the rest of his champagne on my breasts and licking it off.

I got turned on in spite of myself.

"Main Man," he said, "wants to visit every place on your lovely body."

Brent's heat was soaring tonight and when it got like that, he was a really good lover.

Oh, yeah!

That's the thing about lady luck. One never knows when that sistah is going to show her gorgeous face.

Chapter 14

SAUNDRA

There was no one on the stamp line when I hurried into the post office just to see Yero's face.

He was happy at my impromptu visit but too professional to do more than smile as I leaned on the counter.

"Yero, do you realize that human beings are the only animals who choose to drink the milk of another species?"

His eyebrows started to meet. "Yes. We've had that conversation. Is that what you came here to tell me?"

Flustered and near tears, I kept talking. "And do you know that fish have very sensitive and fragile mouths? Careless handling results in broken jaws. So teaching a child that it is okay to drag a living thing out of its home and kill it just for sport is wrong. Tell me that you will never take our little boy fishing, Yero."

Now he looked really worried. "Saundra, what's *really* wrong?"

The tears began to drip but I lowered my voice. "I should have called you after Daddy and I talked about the engagement party but it was all so upsetting."

He looked baffled. "We're having an engagement party?"

"No."

"Excuse me a minute, baby."

I watched as Yero approached one of his coworkers—a middle-aged woman who took one glance at me, murmured some words back to him, and then took his place at the stamp window.

I said hello and backed away.

The next thing I knew, Yero was by my side looking handsome in his light blue postal shirt and navy pants. He gave me a kiss and took me by the hand to a sort of quiet place near the rented mailboxes.

"What's the matter, baby?"

Now I felt silly. He could get fired.

"Saundra, you never come here." He touched my face gently. "And you're crying. Tell me what's made you come unglued."

I told him about Evelyn's suggestion, Daddy's selfish reaction, and how something strange was going on in their relationship. Something that Daddy refused to tell me until after all my special events were over because he knew it would upset me.

"If you want to get your family together, we can do it at my house. Your father can either join us or stay home," Yero answered matter-of-factly. "As far as their relationship is concerned, it really isn't our business. You'll have plenty of time to be upset when he tells you the story. Why waste the precious days and hours that God will hopefully see fit to give you in the meantime?"

"You're right, but I just know the story is something that will hurt Evelyn."

"Baby, Evelyn can take care of herself. Trust me, she'll be fine."

And with Yero's words, the pieces of my world fell back into place.

Chapter 15

SAUNDRA

As I traveled down Guy Brewer Boulevard in a van to the train station, I chose to block out the loud reggae music and the incoherent shouting of the Jamaican driver by looking out the gray tinted windows. The lightning speed of the van and the freezing weather were no match for my wandering thoughts and the flames of passion that burned deep within me.

Yero and I were intimate at his house last night. His mother and younger brother, Khari, went out and we had the rest of the evening to spend quality time together. Sex wasn't planned but I wore my prettiest rose panty and bra set just in case. He had citrus-scented candles strategically placed around his room and a tape with the sounds of a tropical rain playing softly in the background. His strong hands massaged my back and neck as I took in the atmosphere and the feeling of complete surrender to any and every thought. Removing his shirt and then my own, I kissed him passionately, swaying slowly along with the sound of the wind blowing through the trees. Placing his hand gently on my stomach and pulling back the comforter with the other, he guided me to lie down on my back. I will never forget the wonderful sensation of my warm skin pressed against the cool cotton sheets as he gave me a sensuous foot massage. After being pampered and rubbed tenderly with beautifully scented oils, I experienced sexuality so pure, so elevating that I reached levels of consciousness beyond time and space.

Usually with the men I've been with in the past, it was like being in bed with an animal in heat. They clawed, grappled, charged, screamed, and did everything but foam at the mouth. Yero took his time and actually looked into my eyes. At no point did I feel like a nail being hammered into the wall; and that's how it's supposed to be.

Afterwards he held me close and murmured how beautiful I was as he stroked my hair. It sure beat the "I need a cigarette and some sleep" losers of yesteryear.

This is going to be a hectic week for me. I'm organizing a Black Heroes Day celebration for the children at the community center down the block and I have a lot of schoolwork. I was surprised when I was asked to take on the project even though I often stopped by the center and read stories to the kids. I didn't think anyone noticed, nor did I care; the children loved it and that was all that mattered to me. I feel so sorry for some of those kids; most of their parents just sit them in front of the Cartoon Network and let Bugs and Daffy raise them. Or worse, they sit them in front of music videos, complete with materialistic wannabe players and self-proclaimed superfreaks. A couple of months ago I met a little boy who knew the verses of all the latest rap songs but could not recite his times tables. That wasn't cute *at all*.

Although I'm swamped in responsibility, I decided to be supportive of Yero and go out tonight with him, his brother Khari, and Khari's girlfriend, Joanne. Today is Khari's twenty-second birthday and Joanne wants to surprise him with a party at Red Lobster. I'm real cool with Khari and Joanne but the thought of being around all that seafood already makes me nauseous. Even before I became a vegan I couldn't stand the smell of seafood. Hopefully, we won't stay too long.

Joanne told us they'd be at the Green Acres Mall Red Lobster by six-thirty. Of course because of CP time it was now seven-fifteen. We had been seated twenty minutes ago and were tired of picking at bread and listening to the elevator music they provided. Just when Yero was about to start complaining, they came in. Their heads swiveled in an attempt to find us in the crowded room and I motioned to them from our booth in the back.

"Hey!" Khari shouted to us.

I got up to give them hugs and I noticed a small bulge when Joanne opened her coat. Nah, it couldn't be.

"Hi Jo! What's up K; Happy Birthday!" I said, wrapping my arms around them.

"Thanks, sis."

"You're getting old, K," Yero said, giving his brother a pound.

"But I'll always be younger than you," he said, laughing.

Yero chuckled and sipped his glass of water.

"What's new, Jo?" I asked, sitting back down. I looked at her and smiled. I knew what was coming and I hoped Yero wouldn't be too upset.

"Well . . . I'm uh . . . pregnant," she said, blushing down at the tablecloth.

"Pregnant?" Yero said in an hysterical tone.

"That's so nice . . ." I started.

"Fuck, no! Y'all aren't ready for this," Yero said, causing a scene.

Joanne looked shocked at his reaction and turned crimson. Khari grabbed her hand and turned to his brother in fury.

"Damn, Yero, why are you trippin'?"

"Why am *I* trippin'? Because you two need jobs, that's why! I can't believe this shit!"

"First of all, you shouldn't be all up in my shit; we're going to get jobs but it's just going to take a little more effort, that's all."

Joanne still had her head down and I could see her eyes welling up with tears.

"They'll manage, Yero," I said, trying to sound chipper.

"Ah, that's great. Didn't Joanne have an abortion once already?"

We all were horrified by his question and I couldn't believe he said it. Joanne got up and ran to the bathroom Marcia Brady–style.

"I should drop you right now for what you said," Khari said, getting up to get Jo.

"If you feel froggy, then go ahead and leap," Yero said with his arms outstretched. I was appalled by the whole incident. Yero had never acted like this before and I can't believe Joanne has had an abortion. Khari looked at him like he wanted to rip him to shreds but chose to check on Joanne instead.

"You know that was wrong for you to do that, right?" I asked, glaring at him with my arms folded.

"Hell, no! Khari had no business getting Jo pregnant when he knows that neither one of them has any income. Besides, they're both lazy and once the baby gets here Mama will have to do all of the work. She raised her kids already, it's not fair to her."

"I understand all that but it's done now and you should have let it go."

"I'm going to speak my mind. You don't understand Khari like I do. Mama had to pay for Joanne to get the first abortion. We always end up fixing his messes."

"A baby is *never* a mess, Yero," I said softly, looking away.

"You know what I mean," he said, touching my hand, sensing my disappointment in his statement. "I'll love that kid once it gets here but I just wish he would've waited until he could do his thing with a job in his own house."

"I know but let's not discuss this any more tonight. We're supposed to be having a good time. Let's try to salvage what we can of this evening."

He shook his head as if reason was coming back to him.

I got up to see what was happening with Jo and Khari.

As I walked by, a tall white man in a uniform approached me. "Excuse me, miss, but I've been getting complaints from other customers about the noise in your area. If it doesn't stop pronto I'm going to have to ask you to leave."

"I'm sorry but the situation is under control now."

"Alrighty, then," he said, strolling away.

I went to the ladies' room to see what was going on.

Khari was waiting for Jo to come out. His jaw was locked with rage.

"Khari, I'm sure Yero's sorry for what he did; he just wants the best for you guys and it came out the wrong way."

"Nah, that was foul, Saundra; he didn't have to say all that. Fuck him," he said with his voice reaching a high pitch.

"I know you're upset but let's try to have a good time and put this behind us," I reasoned, placing a reassuring hand on his rigid shoulder.

"I'll try for *you* because you're cool but if he says *anything* else I don't like, we're going to have to settle this like gentlemen," he said, pointing towards the parking lot. I laughed at the irony of his statement and shook my head.

"I'm going in to see what Jo's doing," I said, pushing the door open.

"Jo?" I called.

I heard sniveling in the second stall and I sighed in annoyance. "Jo, please come out of the stall. Yero's sorry for what he said. He just doesn't want you guys to end up struggling."

As soon as I finished my sentence, I heard a howl. Oh, no; I was only making things worse.

"Jo, please come out; everything will be fine; I promise."

I heard the latch on the door snap back and she emerged with a puffy red face and her hair flying everywhere.

"Oh, Jo," I said, rushing to hold her. She collapsed into my arms and bawled into my sweater. I tried to put her hair back in place but the moisture from her sweat and tears made it cling to her cheeks and neck like glue.

"Wash your face and let's get out of here all right?"

"Yero hates me and my baby. Oh, God!" she wailed.

"Get a grip; he does not hate you or the baby. He loves you guys and he wants the best for you. He got upset and he said some stupid things."

She went over to the sink and started splashing water on her face. With every handful it looked a little better but her eyes were still swollen. After she brushed her hair and straightened her clothes, we left the bathroom.

"You, OK?" I asked.

"Yeah."

Khari was still waiting outside. We all went back to the table. Yero was sitting there with a pitiful look on his face.

"I'm sorry for that, ya'll. I love you two, you know that, don't you?"

Khari shook his head unimpressed, but Jo managed a weak forgiving smile. A waiter came over and took everyone's order. Things got better once the food and drinks arrived and with Yero's and Khari's sense of humor it's hard to stay angry long. Yero and I had a vegetable plate, Jo had the lobster and Khari had the blue crab. The smell began to make me nauseous but I fought it by taking a gulp of water every time I felt a lump in my throat. I felt woozy with the snap of every leg in front of me and all I could do was smile when something funny was said. Khari picked up the crab and ripped off the upper part of the shell.

The crab looked odd but I couldn't figure out why.

Joanne squinted at it suspiciously. "That's horrible!"

"Ugh!" Khari said, wiping his hands on his napkin.

Yero simply stared in disbelief and looked at me hunched over. As I choked and gagged over the table, the people in the area stared with disgust.

"What happened?" our waiter asked, running up to us in a frenzy.

"You served us a pregnant crab!" Khari exclaimed.

The waiter stared at the plate and his mouth dropped open.

"I'm so sorry; would you like me to get you another, sir?" he said, looking sympathetically at me but directing his question to Khari.

"Hell, no, that's quite all right."

"I'm so sorry. You don't have to pay for this. I'll speak to the manager right away," he said, rushing off.

We watched the busboys scurry around, clearing the table and decided not to eat at all. I was standing up to leave when my cell phone rang. It was Asha, chattering about the latest events in her ridiculous, soap opera life. The only way to get her off the phone was to promise her a visit.

Chapter 16

ASHA

Saundra came over after work. Although we both have pretty faces, looking at the two of us, no one would guess we were sisters. She is tall and dark skinned and while I prefer my sleek page boy hairstyle, she wears hers in shoulder length dreadlocks. But it is the way she dresses that makes me want to run screaming from the room. If she isn't draped in a caftan with clogs on her feet, it is handmade dashikis with sandals or boots.

As she walked into my apartment, the foreign scent she was wearing threatened to overwhelm me.

My nose wrinkled. "What kind of perfume is that?"

"It's cocoa-mango oil."

She sat Indian style on the floor and gave me a beatific smile. It was the kind of grin usually seen on the faces of Moonies, Branch Davidians or other cultists. While I dashed around getting rid of my work gear, she just sat there totally absorbed in knitting something. The needles clicked and some green yarn slowly coiled itself out of her huge handbag. The work caused her many silver bangles to jingle. The folds of her long black cape formed a beautiful umbrella around her and was the perfect base for a forest green and yellow dashiki that she proudly wore with an elaborate matching headwrap. When I dropped my briefcase on the sofa, she lifted her head and exposed her gorgeous set of straight white teeth in a one hundred-watt smile.

"What's up, girl?"

"Randy bought me a dog."

"Aw, that's nice; where is it?"

"I locked him in the bathroom."

"All day? That's horrible!"

"Whatever. That mutt is not tearing up all my shit."

"You're awful."

When I opened the bathroom door, a series of weak yelps indicated my pet had anxiously awaited my arrival.

Saundra immediately snatched him. "He's so cuuute! What's his name?"

"I don't know."

"You gotta give him a name," Saundra declared. "Look at him . . . he's so precious."

"You think of a name while I feed him."

When Saundra gets around animals, she goes nuts. Her house is a combination of Noah's Ark and the botanical fucking gardens.

I couldn't help but smile at the puppy as he scampered around anticipating his meal. "How about Sparky?"

"That's too hard. I want something soft and feminine."

"But it's a boy dog, Asha."

"I don't care. I've just decided that his name is Peaches."

Saundra's mouth twisted in disapproval.

I decided to change the subject. "What are we having for dinner tonight?" I asked.

"Indian, Thai? . . ."

"Chinese. Let me wash up first."

"Can we go to West Fourth Street first?"

I'd been expecting that request. "No."

While I practically live at Bloomingdale's, Saundra always wants to go poking around in some seedy little thrift shops. The girl lives for grandma-length skirts, foreign textiles and eccentric jewelry. It's amazing that just six years ago she used to be a miniskirt and leather pants-wearing club kid who didn't give a damn about anything except having fun. Now she's a spiritually conscious vegan with ancient words of wisdom constantly dripping from her lips.

After showering, I jumped into a pair of tight fitting boot cut jeans and my favorite clingy maroon sweater. I walked back into the living room to put on my boots and was appalled to find Peaches on the couch resting near Saundra.

"What the hell . . . get off the couch!" I screamed and gestured at the scared pooch.

He hopped down and looked at me with confusion.

I saw Saundra's mouth turning down at the corners and I wasn't in the mood for a goddamn PETA speech when this fleabag was on my nice leather couch.

"That was completely unnecessary. He wasn't hurting the couch," she said, snapping her fingers for Peaches to come over to her.

"Whatever. Let's go," I snapped.

"Asha, can I ask you a question?"

I rolled my eyes in frustration because I didn't want my treatment of Peaches to become the subject of the evening. "What?"

"Did you put those jeans on with a spray gun?" She laughed. "You're so silly."

We decided to go to a nice restaurant around the corner from my house.

A couple laughing softly, holding hands and a couple of drunk Mexicans leaving the billiards room were the only people who gave the block life. Next to the Chinese restaurant it was the opposite. A noisy crowd of people was standing on line waiting to get into a karaoke bar next door and some teenagers with a boombox stood in front of a rollerblade shop blasting techno.

To our relief, as soon as the glass doors of the restaurant closed behind us, the noise vanished, leaving us peacefully to the light tinkle of traditional Chinese music. We were greeted cordially by a tiny woman with a short haircut and escorted to a small red booth by the window. The restaurant was dimly lit, warm, and practically empty except for the oil paintings of magnificent pagodas and bronze life-sized statues of ancient Chinese gods.

Saundra and I caught up on three weeks worth of gossip while we ate. As I sipped my tea, I noticed twinkles of mirth in Saundra's dark brown eyes.

"What's on your mind?"

"I'm thinking about how you're using that poor man."

"Randy?"

"Duh, yes, Randy," she said, badly imitating my soft voice with her deep one.

"I don't *use* anybody. I can't help it if men give me things because of the way I look."

"You know you don't care about them but you'll take and take and take. Have you no conscience at all?" Saundra asked as if we hadn't had this dialogue half a dozen times already.

"No, I don't rob or steal. They like giving me things."

"They're giving you those things in the hope of a commitment."

"That's not true in every case. Brent is a married man and Randall would have to be out of his mind to think that I'd be willing to walk into a lifetime of money worries just because he can screw."

"What about Nick?"

I shrugged. "Nick has promised me a beach house. I'll decide what to do about him after I get it."

"You are a walking karma time bomb, you know that."

"Whatever."

I took another sip of my tea and looked at Saundra's soft dark face. It had that *I'm warning you* look on it that she always gave me whenever she saw disaster. Her long ebony locks grazed her shoulders like beautiful threads of yarn. The small silver nose ring and her sterling hoops glimmered with every flicker of the red candle on the table. I decided to speak first so she wouldn't think her threat shook me.

"So how're Phil and Evelyn?"

"They're fine. She still wants to get married but Daddy says that my wedding is enough for him to think about right now."

"How long does she plan to wait? It's been six years and every year Phil comes up with another excuse. She needs to kick his ass to the curb."

"I know."

"Your father is not the type to change without a kick in the ass."

"You got that right," Saundra answered dryly. "He's a stereotypical cop, content with coffee and donuts."

"Phil is built like a tank. It's hard to believe he eats so much junk food," I observed.

"He works hard enough to keep in shape, waking me up with that damn NordicFlex machine."

I daydreamed for a moment about Phil's wonderful body and the crush I used to have on him in high school. He has the most amazing chest, with big muscles and sexy, deep-chocolate skin. When I used to visit Saundra, the highlight was seeing her father in his gray sweatpants lifting his weights, occasionally pouring water over his bald head to keep cool.

"Asha, I need you to help me plan the wedding. Yero and I are going to choose the place but I need a woman's help with all the other stuff."

"What about Evelyn?"

"I want my sister."

She gave me a loving smile and it felt so good that tears pricked the back of my eyelids.

"I want you to be my maid of honor, too. Will you?"

I patted her hand. "Of course, baby."

Maid of honor! I'd have to buy a fabulous dress. Nothing off the rack. It would have to be couture. Who was going to come up with the two or three grand? Brent or Nick?

I was snatched back to reality by a pint-sized waiter shoving a menu in my face.

"I don't need a menu, thanks. I'll have the sweet and sour chicken with white rice," I said, handing it back to him.

"What about your dress?"

"I'm cool. I started sketching some designs for my wedding dress yesterday."

"Lemme guess. It's gonna be made of recycled burlap, a mosquito net for a veil and you'll carry a broccoli stalk bouquet?"

"Oh, you're funny, Ms. Armani. I don't think it'll be that haute couture."

The waiter was looking impatient. "Would you like something to eat, miss?" he asked eagerly, turning to Saundra.

"I'm not sure yet, let me see . . ." Saundra trailed off, wrinkling her forehead in concentration. God does that get on my damn nerves. What the hell is she thinking about! She doesn't *eat* anything. The only choice she can make is to have her seaweed baked or fried.

"I think I'll go with the mixed vegetables, brown rice, and a spring roll without the shrimp." She smiled.

"Why do you do that?" I asked.

"What?"

"You study the menu, *knowing* you're only going to eat vegetables, anyway."

Saundra was exasperated. "I've told you that I'm not going to eat anything that has a face or a spirit. But I still like to know how my vegetables are going to be prepared, so I study the menu." She sighed heavily.

Saundra and I are not as close as we used to be. This type of shit is the reason why.

Chapter 17

SAUNDRA

There's just something about peppermint soap and lavender oil that soothes the soul. The fallen leaves were rustling around outside as I soaked in the bathtub and it reminded me that we would all be turning our watches back in only a week. Soon it would be Halloween. Asha would need me then because it was the one day of the year she found hard to get through. Every trick-or-treater reminded her of the fetus who died six years ago. It was the day her demons danced.

Did Mama do the right thing?

Abortion, except in the case of rape or incest, is wrong. But I understand Mama's fear. She was always preaching to us: Go to college, get established in a profession before you get married, don't depend on the state, relatives or anyone else for money, and never have a baby until your act is together and the foundation of your life is strong. Mama was deathly afraid that one or both of us would turn out like her.

The funny thing is that if mama was alive now, she would be proud of me for earning a bachelor's degree, hate my holistic lifestyle and call me a fool for not chasing the almighty dollar.

Asha has some education, a good job and money in the bank plus her friend Nick took her to a Caribbean resort last week. She called me to say that the place boasted a European spa, golf, scuba diving and eleven gourmet restaurants.

Her cell phone broke a few weeks ago and Brent bought her a new one that makes mine look like a tin can. She said it is a Samsung A670 with both digital and video cameras plus high speed Internet access.

Asha has light skin, a tiny body and small bones just like Mama, but if she were alive, Mama wouldn't approve of Asha, either. The fact that Asha plans to stay single for the rest of her life and never have children would sadden her.

Maybe we can never satisfy our parents.

For example, Daddy has never said a word against Yero and is always kind to him, but I have a sneaking suspicion that he would be happier if I were getting married to someone with a more traditional job. A lawyer, a doctor, or banker.

Maybe we just have to make ourselves happy and let the chips fall where they may.

"Saundra!"

It was Daddy, yelling from upstairs.

"What?"

"Can you come to the phone?"

"Who is it?"

"Yero."

My heart skipped a beat.

"I'll be right down."

I threw my robe on without bothering to dry off, ran down the stairs as fast as I could and picked up the receiver in the living room.

"Hello?"

"Hi, Saundra." His voice sounded dull and tired.

"What's the matter?"

"Joanne had a miscarriage."

"Oh, my God!"

He sighed. "Yeah. Khari just called from the hospital. He is really losing it so I'm going to run over there. Will you come, too?"

I had planned to study all day but Yero needed me.

Chapter 18

ASHA

I woke up this morning feeling blissful until I remembered what day it was. Halloween. My baby had been dead six years. Saundra phoned as if on cue.

"Are you all right?"

"Fine."

"I'll be there in about an hour. Think of something fun to do."

She hung up before I could say "don't bother" like I did every year.

Aaargh! Am I going to be depressed every fucking Halloween for the rest of my goddamned stupid-ass miserable life?

Think of something fun to do.

Yes. It was Saturday so I didn't have to go to work and Saundra had no classes, but SHIT there would be kids in costumes running up and down every street. Little human beings laughing gaily while dressed up as SpongeBob SquarePants, Dora the Explorer, and the Power Puff Girls.

It would be unbearable!

The only reasonable thing to do was spend the day indoors. Shopping. I was an authorized user of Nick's MasterCard. We would hire a limousine and I would lie down in the backseat as it cruised through the streets so I couldn't see the kids in their finery. When the limo stopped in front of a fashionable clothing boutique or shoe store, Saundra could open the door, make sure that there were no tots in sight and we'd run in.

Much to my surprise, Saundra agreed to the plan.

Chloe. I chose a white, waist-length military jacket with navy stripes, oversized buttons and exposed stitching. Saundra just watched.

Hermes. A sepia patch-pocket skirt. Sandra nearly fainted at the five hundred dollar price tag.

Burberry. A silver trench coat. Saundra closed her eyes when I tried to show her the tag.

Saundra wouldn't get anything and that was getting to be a drag so I told her to go home. Refusing to let me mope around the apartment, she agreed to buy some things but only if I used my own credit card and only if it was a regular department store.

She ended up with a new backpack for her school books, a burgundy striped tie for Yero and a royal blue sweatshirt for Phil.

Whatever.

Back at the apartment, she fell asleep. I drank a pint of rum and joined her.

Chapter 19

SAUNDRA

Yero and I were going to look at tuxedos. I had decided on lilac and silver as my wedding colors and he was unhappy at the thought of wearing a lilac cummerbund around his waist. So, we would have to meet somewhere in the middle—find some sort of compromise. I've always heard that wedding preparations can tear a couple apart and I refuse to lose my life partner over something as silly as a piece of fabric.

I had met Yero Brown at a sweet sixteen party for Pastor Hoffman's granddaughter, Sharon. Pastor Hoffman had raised Sharon since she was eight years old when both her parents died in a plane crash. They lived across the street and Sharon was the first neighborhood girl to offer me some help in adjusting to my new school.

Yero was the cutest guy at the party and I wondered why I hadn't seen him in the halls at school.

Evelyn hadn't come into my life yet so I was still pretty wild. At parties, I used to get a guy's attention by walking straight up to him, grabbing his arm and dragging him onto the dance floor. There, he'd be blown away by my impressive dance moves. Yero was not impressed.

He allowed me to lead him onto the floor, moved to the beat

while I shimmied and twirled, then took me back to Sharon without asking for my phone number.

I was leaning against a wall fuming about this to Sharon when Yero sauntered up to us.

"How you doin', Sharon?"

"Fine, Yero. Are you here to babysit Khari?"

Yero?

He laughed. "Something like that."

I turned to walk away.

"Wait a minute, Soul Train. Where you goin'?"

That was funny so I turned around and smiled. "To get some punch."

Sharon pulled my hand. "Yero Brown, this is Saundra Patterson," she said. "Saundra just moved in across the street from me."

"What happened to the cop?"

"I'm his daughter."

"Oh," said Yero. "I guess I'd better hide my stash."

I knew he was only teasing but the remark also let me know why the other teens seemed to be avoiding me at school and around the block.

"Where are you moving from?" he asked.

"Manhattan."

"Well," he said, "welcome to Queens." He grinned at both of us and strolled back into the crowd.

Sharon told me that Yero was two years out of high school and waiting for the post office to call him. He was at the party with his brother Khari who was an eleventh-grader like me because Khari had a bad temper and would fight at the slightest provocation and Yero would keep things calm. The good news: Yero had been an excellent student, was quiet, well-mannered and had always kept at least a part-time job since he was fourteen years old, the age when New Yorkers are eligible for working papers. He was a gentleman and, although he had been seen with girls, they were always from outside the neighborhood. There was no gossip or scandal connected with Yero and his reputation was spotless.

He didn't approach me again and when the party ended, I

went back across the street feeling very let down. It would have been nice to have a new boyfriend to go along with my new home and my new status as the only female in my daddy's house.

The next day I walked out of the school and turned left toward home, wondering what to do with the rest of my afternoon. I was thinking about how much I already missed Asha when a car rolled up behind me and a male voice called out.

"Saundra!"

I turned around. It was Yero, leaning out of the driver's side window. "

"Hi, Soul Train," he said, grinning. "Come take a ride with me!"

I jumped in and we drove all over Queens, not wanting to leave each other after the conversation started flowing. We rode, stopped for burgers and fries, rode some more and talked about a whole lot of stuff: his mom, who struggled to raise five children after his father ran off with a white nurses' aide; my dad, who was overjoyed that we were finally going to live under the same roof; how he aced the postal exam; my dream of studying fashion design; and how we both used to smoke weed but now thought that drug dealers should all be arrested and charged with attempted murder.

Four hours later, he finally pulled up in front of my house and turned off the ignition. "Saundra, I know this is going to sound crazy but you're the girl I've been looking for. Will you have me?"

Have him? Well, I hadn't had sex since Mama died and I did like Yero Brown an awful lot.

"Yes, but not at my place. If Daddy caught us, he would shoot you and probably throw me in jail till my eighteenth birthday. Is there a hotel nearby?"

"No," said Yero, laughing heartily. "I didn't mean sex. I want to be your boyfriend."

Embarrassed at the fact that I'd been willing to give it up so quickly, I tried to recapture some shred of dignity. With my nose in the air, I rattled off my phone number. "Call me and we'll see," was my answer.

Now, six years later, Sharon Hoffman was a senior at a college in Arizona and Yero and I were headed for the tuxedo shop to look for a cummerbund that Yero would feel comfortable in at our wedding.

Chapter 20

PHIL

I watched as Hugo, my short and stocky partner of more than ten years, paced in front of my desk. His skin seemed even whiter than usual and he kept ruffling his thinning mop of jet black hair. There was no point in telling him to calm down. Hugo worked out the tension that was part of our job in his own way. We both jumped when the phone rang.

"Detective Patterson," I said.

It wasn't the call we'd been waiting for.

"Phil, I need a favor."

"Spit it out, James. I don't have much time."

David James was a fellow detective who had a serious gambling problem. He was always coming up short on cash and I had a bad habit of helping him out.

"Can you let me hold a hundred dollars till next Tuesday?"

"Yeah. Fine."

"You sound pissed off, man. Look, this is the last time."

"I'm under a lot of pressure right now, James. Gotta go."

"Can I pick up the money right now?"

"Yeah, man."

I hung up before he could thank me. Hugo and I were waiting for a call from one of our snitches. We'd been waiting a long time—she was supposed to check in more than an hour ago. If she came through, we might take down one of the busiest crack dealers in the area. If she chickened out, we had lost a whole lot of man hours and a few hundred dollars that belonged to the NYPD. The boss wasn't going to be happy.

The next call was from the boss. He barked out some orders.

I gave Hugo the thumbs down sign and he groaned.

"We'll be there in a flash, sir."

"You have five minutes."

The captain hung up without another word. I grabbed my jacket and Hugo raced toward his desk to retrieve his own.

"Where we goin'?" asked Hugo.

I didn't answer him until we were out of the precinct and on the road. "We got a body in Laurelton. Woman says she came in and found it . . . doesn't know whodunit."

Hugo groaned. "Why did I become a cop?"

I had to laugh. When shit got too thick, Hugo and I had this routine that we did.

"Same reason I did. To protect the good people from the bad people."

"Who are the bad people?"

"Rapists, burglars, murderers and drug dealers."

"How do you tell the difference?"

"We can't. So fuck it. Let's lock everybody up and figure it out later."

Sometimes the cops are the bad guys. That is an unfortunate reality. But Hugo and I were both clean. It's really sad that the bad cops get so much ink in the newspapers because they are the minority. We've never even taken a free cup of coffee or a donut. We're old-fashioned, honest cops and proud of it. So we rode through the busy streets of Queens in our black unmarked vehicle hoping that the woman who called about a dead body would just confess to the goddamn crime and save us a whole lot of trouble.

"Did you buy a Lotto ticket this week?"

"Nah," answered Hugo. "You?"

"Hell, yeah. Something told me that the bitch was going to

flake out on us. I'm going to need that Lotto money after unemployment runs out."

"We should find her and kick that ass."

Hugo was always talking about kicking ass but he never really did it. In fact, neither of us has ever used excessive force on a snitch or a suspect. We're proud of that, too.

I turned right onto what was normally a quiet block. It was crowded with crying people, nosy people and stunned people. Uniformed police officers kept them all behind the yellow crime scene tape. We showed our identification and entered the house.

The woman who had made the call, a Miss Jane Hunter, was a slim, attractive black woman in her late twenties. She wore a typical ghetto hairdo—twirled and gelled into a towering structure about eight inches from her scalp. Her makeup was streaked with tears. We questioned her for about ten minutes about the covered body of a black teenage male in the kitchen. Everything that came out of her mouth was a lie.

We finally gave her the right to remain silent spiel, slammed the cuffs on and hauled her ass back to the precinct.

There was a coded message waiting for me. It meant that our snitch had called with the information we needed. Our jobs weren't on the line after all.

Chapter 21

EVELYN

I had just finished twisting a gorgeous swath of turquoise fabric into a turban around my head when Hugo called. I knew right away what that meant. Phil had decided to pull a double shift and his partner had agreed to take me out instead.

"Hi, Evelyn. How would you like to keep a short Puerto Rican man company this evening?"

Hugo and I had been friends since our days at the police academy . . . long before he introduced me to Phil. "So he is doing a midnight to eight, huh?"

"Yeah, *chica.* Our boy has some heavy-duty expenses coming up. *Comprende?*"

It was true. Saundra's wedding. Saundra's boutique. Our wedding. And Phil knew that I was making my career change right after we tied the knot. The retreat for women would satisfy my soul but my paycheck would be a lot smaller. How could I get mad?

"I'd love to have dinner with you, Hugo. It will give us a chance to catch up."

"Good!" He sounded genuinely pleased. "I'll take you anywhere you want to go, but I have three conditions."

"What are they?"

"The food must be cooked . . . nothing raw, like sushi. They must serve meat even though you aren't going to eat any of it."

"What is the third?" I already knew but he really wanted to say it.

"They have to have a real bar. No spritzers. No wine coolers. I want Jack Daniel's both straight up and on the rocks."

"So, I have to watch you keel over with a massive heart attack? That's not my idea of fun, Hugo."

"What if I promise not to collapse until you're back home? My living room is huge. Plenty of room for me to lie facedown until the medics arrive."

I had to laugh. "Suit yourself."

"Good! See you in a few minutes."

I hung up, poured myself a glass of organic apple juice and stared out my bedroom window. It was dusk—a crisp autumn evening with a slight wind that was blowing the red and gold leaves around on our lawn. I wondered if my first husband, Jerry Turner, still lived in New York City. We had promised each other all the usual things: remain friends, stay in touch, blah, blah, blah; but after all the drama died down, there really wasn't anything more to say. We were just kids when we got married, and after it was over, I couldn't afford to keep the apartment. Not on a McDonald's cashier's salary. Besides, we'd had so many hopes and dreams there. I just didn't want to look at the space where we had placed the crib or inside the drawers that held stacks of baby clothing from the shower that Mama and Josephine had thrown for me. So, when Mama suggested I move back home and take a bunch of tests to land a city job, I figured she was right.

That's one thing about Mama: she keeps moving forward and never looks back. Dad was a sanitation worker and one night he had an asthma attack and died. I was a ten-year-old—away at summer camp. When the counselor told me, I was stunned—too lost to even cry until many years later. He had been a wonderful father and I adored him. Maybe I didn't cry because mama didn't dwell on it. She used the life insurance money to pay off the mortgage on our house and kept on working at the nursing home where she'd been the resident dietician for years. She still works there part time, even though she retired many years ago.

I took every test that the City of New York had to offer that year and the New York Police Department was the only organization that showed interest. So, I jumped at the chance to earn a good salary and benefits. The notion of good vs. evil never even entered my thoughts. These days, you can't get on the force without a college degree but back then all you needed was a high school diploma.

Hugo and I were the only minorities in the academy that year and he helped me through the grueling physical challenges. What a nice guy! I wish he would find a nice woman, settle down and have kids. I've been to several of his family parties and he really has a kind and gentle way of dealing with children. But Hugo says he doesn't ever want to get married. He has his little bachelor pad in Manhattan and a very simple life that seems to make him happy.

Boy, when Hugo and I first joined the force, we had some grand old times. We'd go out after our shift was over and drink ourselves silly. In fact, I used to be able to out-drink Hugo. The hard stuff. Rye. Scotch. Whiskey. It didn't matter. We would go someplace with loud, live music and get totally wasted to shut out the eight hours of human misery that we had just shoveled our way through. Our friendship didn't change until I met this guy named Miles Galloway. He was a high school math teacher. A deep man who lived a holistic lifestyle that I didn't understand at first. But the more I fell in love with him, the more I was eager to learn. He introduced me to yoga, meditation, veganisim and various eastern philosophies. The relationship lasted two years and ended when he asked me to quit the force. At the time, I was too afraid to leave. Where else was I going to make such good money with only a twelfth grade education? Miles said that if I still cared about money, then I hadn't totally thrown off my shackles. He wouldn't have minded my working if the job didn't involve guns, violence, and some laws that are just plain unfair. I understood where he was coming from but what if we didn't work out? I visualized myself back at the McDonald's counter and let Miles Galloway depart in peace.

Meanwhile, Hugo had won kudos for risking his life in the line of duty. He had also become a savvy political animal and was now Detective Hugo Montana while I was still pounding the pavement in a blue uniform. That's fine.

We all have our place in the universe.

Chapter 22

ASHA

Randy wants me to spend Thanksgiving with him and his family. I'm nervous. He bought me a cuddly pet, now he wants me to meet a mother that even *he* hardly sees. These are clear indications that he's getting serious and that's exactly what I *don't* want.

I took the day off from work today and I'm glad I did. The rain was hitting the pavement like a ton of bricks and the constant honking of the car horns outside indicated that the traffic was hell. I'm recuperating from another wild all-night sex-fest with Nick. I told Randy I stayed home because I felt a slight case of the sniffles. He said he'd be over later to check up on me. *Great,* I thought, *now I have to waste* real *energy faking a fucking cold.* I watched the *Price Is Right* and realized in disbelief that I was genuinely entertained. That is *frightening* and I am so glad I don't do this every day. Just as I was cursing out a fat, hunched over, blue-haired old lady for winning a sports car, the doorman knocked.

"Yes?" I shouted.

"Delivery, Miss Mitchell."

"Just a minute," I responded, as I pulled my red satin robe together.

When I opened the door, he was balancing a long white box in his left hand and shoving a clipboard at me with his right.

"Sign here," he said, pointing with his pen to the only free space on the page. I snatched the pen out of his hand. I hate when people instruct me on the obvious, like I don't have eyes to see a big-ass red X in bold marker.

"Thanks," I said, grabbing the box from his hand.

"No. Thank *you*," he said eyeing my breasts that were spilling out of the Satih robe.

I closed the door without giving him a tip. Normally, I'll give him five dollars for bringing something upstairs, but I only had a one hundred dollar bill in the house.

As I rushed toward the couch with the box, I managed to kick over the glass of grapefruit juice I had been sipping from all morning. That didn't matter right now; I had to see what was inside. Flipping the top on the floor, I discovered two dozen yellow, long-stemmed roses resting neatly on top of one another. They were soft and fragrant. I picked up the accompanying note nestled between the leaves.

It read:

> *I hope these roses*
> *brighten your gloomy day.*
> *Get well soon.*
> *Love, Randy*

Shit. Now he was sending me flowers because of a cold. This was getting way out of hand. Something had to be done and *fast.* He would have to get cut off after Thanksgiving so he could heal in time for Christmas.

I ended up sleeping the rest of the day and only woke up when a cousin called. She wanted to know what my plans were for Thanksgiving. I told her I was going to Randy's mother's house for dinner. God, I hate the holidays; you have to sit in a scorching-hot living room with family members you don't see at any other time of the year, a fake smile plastered on your face. Not only that, you have to deal with rambunctious male relatives whooping and hollering over the football game as they throw cans of beer down their throats. Thank goodness, the only family Randy has is his mother, sister, and niece. I *definitely* wouldn't go if I had to be inspected by a house full of people just for a dried up piece of turkey.

Randy arrived at about ten P.M., while I was finishing a TV dinner. Peaches started to bark when he heard the doorman's buzzer and I quickly began doing jumping jacks so I could get hot and flushed. I repeatedly rubbed my nose as hard as I could with the back of my hand so it would look red and bulbous. A couple of pieces of what appeared to be snotty tissues by the sofa was the grand finale. I told the doorman to let him up.

Randy knocked on my door three times and I got up on the fourth, to milk my "illness" for all it was worth.

"Hi, Bandy," I said, faking a nasal voice.

"My poor baby. I bought you some chicken noodle soup and some saltine crackers," he said, placing a brown paper bag in my hands.

"Dank you berry much. And danks for the blowers. Dey are bootiful."

"No problem."

Peaches ran to Randy with his tale wagging furiously back and forth in a friendly gesture.

"Hey, boy, how you doin?" he said, reaching down for his head.

After putting the bag down on the kitchen counter, I took his wet coat and umbrella and hung them up in the bathroom.

"Do you feel any better than you did this morning?"

"Yeah, I slept all day."

"That's good. You think you'll be well enough by Thursday? I really want you to meet my mother."

"Sure. I'll just have to dose up damorrow and Wednesday."

"Do you need anything from the store? I have to get some work done on my computer at home tonight, but I'll run out first if you need me to. You shouldn't go out in this weather."

"Nah, I'll be albight. You get going; it's going to be hard to catch a cab."

"I feel bad leaving you in this condition but I have a very important deadline to make; please forgive me," he said, getting his things out of the bathroom.

"Don't burry about it. I'll see you on Dursday."

"OK."

Two minutes after I closed the door behind him, he knocked again. He was always forgetting something.

"Yeah?" I asked.

"It's me."

I opened the door and he stood there in his soggy wool coat with a corny smile on his face.

"I just came back to tell you I love you."

He kissed me gently on the lips then bolted without giving me a chance to utter a sound. My heart ached as he said those dreadful words and I wanted him out of my life as soon as possible. I sat down on the floor next to Peaches and contemplated my strategy.

Thanksgiving morning was a nightmare. All my cousins began calling me at the crack of dawn, showering me with good holiday wishes. I spoke to those who have interesting lives and left my machine on for the others. They were my dad's people and maybe I should be grateful that they wanted to keep in touch—we just don't have much in common. I called Saundra even though she doesn't celebrate "exploitive European holidays."

"Hello?"

It was dumb-ass Evelyn. Was she going to grow old waiting for Phil to change his mind?

"Hi, Evelyn. Its Asha."

"Sweetie! How is life treating you?"

"Fine. What is new in your world?"

She laughed, a soft tinkling sound. "Wondering how we're going to pull off a big graduation party in June and a wedding eight weeks later. Whew! It makes me tired just thinking about it."

"Graduation party?"

"Yes. Phil wants her to have both."

Oh, brother! Now he had a believable excuse for not marrying her ass next year. He would say that he didn't have the money and didn't want her to foot the bill alone. How could she deal with the bullshit?

"Is Saundra home?"

"Uh . . . sure."

I knew that she was hurt by my abruptness, but stupid women get on my nerves.

Saundra picked up with Jamiroquai playing loudly in the background. I hate Jamiroquai.

"Hi, Ashie," she said playfully.

"What's new?" I asked.

"A lot, but you don't know how to call nobody?" Saundra said in a ghetto-type voice.

"You got my number," I said.

"You tell me your dirt first and then I'll tell you mine."

"On Sunday Nick came over because he was in town visiting some friends and he dropped by to see me before he left on Monday morning."

"Uh-huh," she said, as if she already knew the rest.

"And we ended up throwing down all night long," I said excitedly.

"That's foul but you are a female Mack, complete with the big brim. Whoa, wah, wow." She laughed, imitating the wa-wa pedal from the seventies.

"I am not! I learned it from watching you back in the day."

"Don't even try it. So what else happened?"

"I took the day off because I was so worn out and Nick didn't leave until seven. I told Randy I took the day off because I had a cold. You should've seen me dart around here trying to look sick when he came over!" I laughed.

"You are too much." Saundra chuckled. "Are you spending Thanksgiving with him?"

"Yeah, unfortunately. He wants me to meet his mama."

"Where does she live?"

"Up in Harlem on 145th and Lenox"

"Yikes, that's *Good Times* area," she said, snickering.

I laughed at the comparison, hoping his mother did not look like the late Esther Rolle.

"I don't know, but I'm no dumb thrill seeking teenager anymore. Slums are not my favorite place to be," I said, grabbing a bottle of clear nail polish off the nightstand.

"Smart choice," Saundra agreed.

"So what's your news?" I said, doubting it's juiciness.

"Me and Yero picked out our wedding bands and auditioned a jazz trio."

"I thought you didn't have *time* to plan a wedding," I mocked.

"Well things just sort of worked out that way." Saundra sighed peacefully.

The phone beeped on my other line. "Saundra, I'll speak to you later, that's probably Randy."

"Let me know what happens in the hood," she teased.

I laughed and clicked over.

The ride uptown was terrible. Not only did it take us forever to find a cab to go to Harlem, the driver barely spoke English. His dark red turban shook affirmatively with every question asked of him and he continued to check his rearview mirror to pulse the level of Randy's and my frustration. After circling one particular row of condemned houses for the thousandth time, Randy and I decided to walk. We would rather take the chance of a possible tangle with some crackheads than *knowing* we were going to go to jail for killing Rahij Singh.

We were only two blocks away from his house and I felt horrified and dismayed with every sound of empty crack vials crunching loudly under my heeled feet. It was an unusually warm day for the middle of November and, of course, that meant every snaggletoothed drunk was out, lying about their glorious pasts. Randy looked a little embarrassed that some spoke and even referred to him as the "Lil' Thompson boy."

The tenement he grew up in was filthy and decayed. It appeared to have been a rust color, but time and negligence made even that indecipherable. Even the couple of stray dogs nearby seemed lifeless and without hope. I had to admire Randy for being where he is today after seeing such depression day in and day out.

The air inside the building was thin and stale. It smelled like everything that had happened in the building in the last thirty years. The odors from the new Thanksgiving meals being cooked were destined to become added to the decayed old stench.

The sounds of the staticky TVs, blaring radios, and laughter ricocheted off the thin walls as we creaked up the stairs. When we approached his mother's door on the third floor, we both began adjusting ourselves to be more presentable. He knocked on a door with a small metal latch attached to the peephole and we heard a little girl with a raspy voice ask who it was.

"That's my niece." Randy grinned.

When she opened the door I almost fainted. She was the ugliest little thing I ever saw. No more than seven years old, she had mounds of fat that caused her eyes to chink up from the pressure. Her cheeks hung down like the jowls on a bulldog. A ruffly, flower print dress didn't help and the ghetto hairdo wouldn't have been complete if her mother hadn't put *the whole pack* of barrettes on her two inches of hair.

"Uncle Randy!" she said, opening her arms for a hug.

"How's uncle's princess?" he exclaimed.

Princess? I wondered as I looked at the blob.

I quickly scanned the room and it was nice and clean for where his mother lived. Pictures in vintage wooden frames aligned the walls and her aged dining room table sat proudly in the center of the room. A centerpiece was attempted with a tacky arrangement of discount store plastic flowers.

"Hi. My name is Alize," she said, smiling, extending her chubby little hand.

"I'm Asha, and how are you doing?"

"Fine. Happy Thanksgiving."

The whole time we were standing there, Randy stared at this kid as if she was a jewel. I struggled to hold back my disgust. Simply looking at that child should be enough reason for condom usage.

"Where's Mommy and Nana?" he asked.

"They're in the kitchen," she said, skipping into one of the back rooms.

"Asha, you want something while I'm in the kitchen?"

"No, thanks."

When he passed through the long amber-colored beads that led into the kitchen, I heard an uproar of joyous greeting from his mother. I took off my coat and laid it down on a stray chair next to the antique grandfather clock. As I began looking at family pictures, a thin, gray-haired woman with a warm smile approached me.

"Asha, I'm junior's mother. It's so wonderful to finally see your face," she said, giving me a hug.

"Nice to meet you too, Ms. Thompson," I said, flashing my brightest smile.

"You're so pretty, now I know why junior's been so crazy about you."

I smiled uneasily at the sound of the man I sleep with being referred to as "junior."

"Make yourself at home. I'm putting the finishing touches on dinner right now." She beamed and went back into the kitchen. I heard heavy footsteps behind me and I turned around. What I met was a three-hundred-pound, high-yellow woman wearing a bright orange spandex and a Little Kim T-shirt.

"You must be Velma," I said, smiling.

"Yeah, who are you?" she said, beating the flour off her humongous thighs, sizing me up.

"I'm Asha, your brother's friend."

"Never heard of you, but hi," she said, waddling into the kitchen.

I stared sorrowfully at her blonde finger-waved head, which looked minuscule in comparison with her enormous bulk. She also had a mug on her, not as bad as her daughter, Alize, but she was definitely a runner-up.

It amused me to see pictures of Randy's evolution from infancy to adulthood but one in particular interested me. It was a photo of Randy and a pretty, light-skinned girl with long black hair. It said "Forever" on the bottom in pink bubble letters with a thin paper frame like it was taken at a fair. They were obviously in love because he was gazing at her the same way he looks at me now. I was curious to find out why they broke up, to see if there was a way I could repeat whatever went wrong.

Velma thundered back into the room and stood there eyeballing me again. It was now obvious that she's one of those fat chicks who can't stand thin women, so I had to flatter her to get the information I wanted. I quickly remembered seeing an awful picture of her at a prom with her pitifully scrawny-looking date. They looked like the simp and the blimp, but I could tell by her facial expression in the shot that she thought they had it going on.

"You looked really nice at your prom, what year was that?"

"Thank you, I think it was '81, when the Sugarhill Gang was big."

"Mmm."

"So what you do?" she said, sitting down on one of the dining room chairs.

"I'm an accessories buyer at Macy's."

"Was dat?" she retorted with her face twisted.

"It's when you choose wallets and belts for . . ."

"You make a lot of money?"

"I do okay," I answered, appalled by her lack of class.

"You think you can hook me up? I'm tired of being on welfare, they hassle me so."

"You ever worked in a store before?"

"Kentucky Fried Chicken, but that was only for the summer while my friend Kiki had her baby."

"Mmm-hmm."

Just when I was going to run out screaming, leaving a bodyprint through the wall like a cartoon character, Randy and Ms. Thompson emerged with platters of food. It smelled great and I looked forward to a nice meal after such a tough journey.

"Alize! Ms. Thompson screamed.

"Alize, the food is ready!" Velma bellowed, obviously knowing how to summon her youngster.

Alize appeared rapidly with the mention of feeding her fat little face. Randy and his mother returned to the kitchen.

"Who's that girl with Randy in the picture up there?" I asked, pointing in its direction.

Her big round face crept towards me as if she was going to tell me her deepest darkest secret.

"That was Randy's fiancée, Tracy. She died just a couple of weeks after that picture was taken."

"What happened to her?"

"She was in a car accident while she was visiting her folks in Michigan. Skull was all crushed up and shit, couldn't even open the casket at the funeral."

Oh, well, I thought. *So much for copying the ex.*

"I thought my brother was goin' to die, too, when it happened. It took him a long time just to get out bed. But I didn't like that bitch or her family anyway. I hate those light-skinned people. They think they're better than everyone."

I shook my head in disbelief. The accident was bad enough but her disrespect for the dead girl shocked me.

"That's terrible," I said, looking at the photo again.

"Don't mention it, though. He gets all funny when we talk about her and it ain't worth his attitude."

"No problem."

I noticed Alize's facial expression as me and Velma talked, and she was stiff as a board. She didn't look remotely alive *until* they brought out the food. I felt kind of sorry for her because it was obvious she was eating to cover some deeper emotional turmoil. Being named Alize was bad enough.

I couldn't wait to get home to call Saundra and tell her what happened. It was killing me that her phone was busy, so I had to dial *66 to get a ring back when she was off the phone. The Pattersons are the only people I know who have not taken advantage of call waiting. Phil's philosophy is that if you want to talk to him that bad, you'll wait. I guess he's right, but they really need to come into the twenty-first century.

In the meantime I decided to catch up on all the latest music videos on BET. After thirty-two minutes and nine seconds of watching young girls thrust their stuff in my face, the phone rang. I picked up the phone and waited to hear Saundra's voice.

"Hello?" Saundra answered.

"Who the hell were you talking to? I've been trying to reach you for two hours!" I said.

"I was on the phone with Yero, but never mind that, give me all the details."

"Well, his mom lives in a dump surrounded by crack dealers, crack whores, and crack heads."

"Uh-huh."

"But she's a real sweet woman and the food was really good."

"What did she look like?"

"Medium height, thin, short gray hair and glasses. She is a cute older woman, but you can tell she was beautiful when she was young."

"Did she like you?" she asked eagerly.

"Like me? She's practically got a wedding dress ironed out! She wouldn't stop asking when we're getting married. I wanted to kick the hell out of her every time she said it."

"What did you say?"

"I just grinned because I knew Randy was behind it all. His sister, now that's a piece of work."

"Was she pretty?"

I immediately burst out laughing and pardoned my sister for her sin.

"I have to spell out what she looked like: S-L-O-T-H."

Saundra laughed out loud. "Damn, you're so mean. I bet she was a little chubby and you just took it there."

"No. She was a sow and her hair had so much gel and grease in it, it had the consistency of papier-mâché.' "

"Oh, no! She had a ghetto do?"

"It was ghetto *before* the blonde dye and sparkles; now it's *alive*."

"Please stop, you're hurting me." She laughed, sounding like she was in pain.

"But that's not it, she has a daughter named Alize."

"Alize? As in the liquor Alize?"

"Yup."

"Did she have a reason for doing that to her child?"

She said she's always liked the finer things in life and she wanted her daughter to have a French name."

"I'm really sorry to hear that; it's so ridiculous" Saundra said. "Is she a nice kid?"

"I guess so. Every time I tried to talk to her, she was shoving a piece of ham in her mouth."

"Gross."

"But that's not the exclusive. Randy's sister told me that he had a fiancée who died three years ago in a car crash."

"Mmm. That's deep," Saundra remarked. "How long were they going together?"

"She didn't say."

"Aw, that's so sad."

"Well it's convenient for me because I'm going to tell Randy that Velma told me about her, and that I don't want to compete with a ghost, so I have to break up with him."

"You've stooped low before but now you've reached a whole other level," Saundra replied. "How could you use something like that against him? He's probably still healing."

"Well then I'm not *causing* him any pain. If he's still going through the motions about some other chick, he'll quickly forget about me."

"That sucks, Asha, and I think you're way out of hand this time," Saundra said with obvious distaste.

"Why are you getting all bent out of shape? You usually hate the guys I date."

"I dislike their arrogance but I don't think Randy deserves what you're going to do to him. He's different."

"Whose side are you on, anyway?" I asked, getting defensive.

"The victim's, of course," Saundra said snottily.

"I'll talk to you later," I said, slamming the phone down.

I should have known better than to tell Saundra my plan. She's always trying to give me some fucking moral lesson every time I do something that she doesn't agree with. Her job is to be my sister, not a therapist nor a counselor; if I need either, I *have* the goddamn yellow pages. Regardless of her opinion, the shit is going down tonight. By this time next week, Randy Thompson should be just another face in my photo album.

*   *   *

I enjoyed my last date with Randy. We went to my favorite Japanese restaurant and after that, we ate chocolate fondue at a French café around the corner. It was truly a fun and delicious evening. Too bad it would end on a sour note. We took a cab to my house but stopped at the liquor store first for some gin. Randy was already a little buzzed from drinking all that sake at the Japanese restaurant, but I needed him drunker so the news wouldn't hurt so much.

Two hours and four drinks later, I knew it was time. I had to stop now and tell him before he passed out or was too incoherent to understand me. Miles Davis filled the candlelit room with his soothing rhythm and I sat down next to Randy on the couch as he smiled at me and tapped his glass to the beat.

"Randy, I have something serious to discuss with you," I said, turning my body completely in his direction.

Usually those words would send alarm signals to someone but the gin made him completely oblivious.

"What's up, baby doll?" he asked, taking another gulp.

"Yesterday Velma told me about your fiancée Tracy, and . . . and I feel like I've sort of taken her place or I'm competing with a ghost," I said, fidgeting with my hands.

His face had an eerie shadow over it at the mention of her name and he stared ahead as if I wasn't there.

"I don't know how to tell you this but I . . . I can't be with you anymore." When I said it, his glass hit the floor sending its remains flying everywhere.

"Asha, please don't do this to me. I love you. I can't believe you would feel as though I'm trying to make you someone else. Velma had no right telling you my business," he said, grabbing for my hand. I jerked away and got up to get the broom.

"I loved Tracy with all my heart and I'm not going to lie to you about that, but I found you and you haven't *replaced* Tracy. You gave me another chance to love," he said, his voice trembling.

I felt that my lie was failing and that a bit of the truth needed to be added in. God, I'm glad I didn't have too much to drink because I probably would've taken it all back.

"Randy, that's not my only problem. You're getting way too serious. I never indicated at any time that I even *wanted* to be loved. All I wanted was to have a good time and have some company. Please understand that I'm not ready for all this."

"Asha, I'm sorry for any stress I've put you through but when I fell for you, I fell so hard. We can take it slow from now on but I'm begging you not to just write me off," he said with tears streaming down his face.

"I can't, Randy. I think it's best if we move on," I said, sweeping up the glass.

"I can't believe you're doing this to us. I thought . . . I mean, I tried to do everything in my power to make you happy," he said, holding his head in his hands.

"Please, Randy, I don't want you to beat yourself up over this. You're a wonderful man and I'm sure there's someone out there who's ready for a commitment."

"Is there someone else?" he asked with his eyes squinted in pain.

"No, I just made a decision," I said, looking him in the eyes.

He put his head down for a brief second and then looked back up at me. "So there's absolutely nothing I can . . ."

"No, Randy, please. I think you should go," I said sternly, cutting him off.

As he got up and walked towards the coatrack his head was hung low in sadness; and what usually was his outstanding posture bore a striking resemblance to the shape of a hunchback. I walked ahead of him and began unlocking the door.

"Take care," I said.

He went out the door and stood there. Why this man was a glutton for punishment, I did not know. Slowly I began to close the door, looking at him in utter confusion.

"I love you," he mouthed silently, with the tears continuing to come down.

I shut the door and went back to Miles and the rest of my gin.

The next two weeks were absolute hell. Randy kept calling, leaving whining messages on my answering machine and filling up my voice mail at work every day. He sent flowers, candy, and gifts, begging me to come back to him, and it drove me up the wall. To make matters worse, he looked up Phil's number and called Saundra, sobbing and pleading for her to talk to me. That was a big mistake, I *was* starting to feel sorry for the guy but calling my sister to complain when we weren't even a committed couple just did not make sense and it made me furious. I had to deal with Saundra's reprimands for days.

Chapter 23

SAUNDRA

What goes around comes around, and one of these days Asha will get her comeuppance. I just hope that her face doesn't need radical reconstructive surgery after it happens.

I told Daddy about Asha's latest adventure over breakfast one morning.

"I'm so afraid that one of these men is going to hurt her."

Daddy took a bite of his buttered toast and chewed it thoughtfully before answering. "Don't worry, sweetheart. Someday she'll meet the right guy and change so fast it'll take your breath away."

Since I'd totally given up on the engagement party idea, the tension had been erased between me and Daddy.

"But in the meantime . . ." I persisted.

He shrugged. "Just keep praying for her."

I nodded and scooped up a melon ball.

Daddy grinned mischievously. "Hugo and I bought you a wedding present."

"So soon? What is it?"

"Remember that reception hall you crossed off your list because it was too expensive?"

Yero and I had checked it out a week ago. It cost $250 per person.

"The Crystal Palace?" I whispered.

"Yup!"

"Oh, Daddy, you shouldn't have. That's way too much money."

"Hugo and I are going to split it. So it's all yours, sweetheart. We paid for one hundred people and an open bar. What do you think of that?" He grinned broadly, looking very pleased with himself.

I rushed around the table, grabbed his face with both hands and kissed him squarely on the forehead. "I think you're the most wonderful father in the world."

Daddy coughed to hide his emotion. "Go on now! Call Hugo and thank him, too!"

Chapter 24

PHIL

The last thing I needed was a fight with Hugo, but he had been sulking around all week and by Saturday afternoon, it was clear to me that he needed to have his say. Hugo was cleaning his already spotless studio apartment while I sat on his turquoise sofa and played a game of solitaire on the heart-shaped glass coffee table.

"When Saundra called to thank me for chipping in on that reception hall, I almost told her the truth myself," Hugo ranted. "This situation has been way out of hand for years but now you're headed for disaster."

I flipped over a card. It was the queen of spades. I had been hoping for a king of diamonds. "Damn!"

Hugo sprayed glass cleaner all over one of his mirrored walls and started rubbing it vigorously with a balled up piece of newspaper. "The Crystal Palace. Saundra's boutique. Evelyn's retreat. Where is all this money supposed to come from?"

"I haven't said anything to Evelyn yet."

"But we both know that you're going to spring that wonderful surprise on her any day now. You are going to tell her that you'll pay for half of what she needs to open that retreat, won't you Phil?"

"Don't worry about it. That won't come out of your pocket."

"You goddamn right, it won't. We've been friends a long time, Phil, but your plan is stupid and it won't work. So, I'm pulling out of it. The Crystal Palace is the last straw. It's where I draw the line."

I was beginning to get heated. "Cut it, Hugo."

"You can go into debt all you want and spread around all the money you want and in the end, the shit is still going to hit the fan. Why can't you see that?"

I responded to that by sweeping up the cards, shuffling them hard and starting a new game.

Hugo continued his tirade as I tuned him out and dealt myself seven cards. By the time I flipped over three kings, he had pulled out the vacuum cleaner and turned it on. The noise really fucked with my concentration. He pushed the machine back and forth across the squeaky clean carpet. He was waiting for me to blow up and start yelling. It was this type of shit that caused a good percentage of the domestic violence cases and dead bodies that I had come across in my career.

In fact, it was probably some silly incident like this that caused old man Willis to hit his wife in the face with a heavy ashtray back when I was a kid growing up in Dayton, Ohio. She came screaming over to our house with blood streaming from her nose. Mom couldn't believe that the mild mannered janitor who worked side by side with Dad at our elementary school could suddenly explode in violence. While Mom put ice on Mrs. Willis's nose, she issued a command to Dad, who was standing there, his mouth open in shock.

"Maxwell, go across the street and see if old man Willis done lost his mind."

Dad's jaw finally started working. "Clara, I ain't going nowhere up in nobody else's business. If you want me to call the cops, fine. They get paid to go ask him questions. I don't."

All the commotion had awakened my three little brothers— Elwood, David, and Buster. Our little family stood on the porch and watched as old man Willis went off to jail and his wife was taken to the hospital.

I hadn't seen my family in a long, long time. The thought

made a lump rise up in my throat and I needed Hugo to stop vac-
uuming and take my mind off them.

"You working tonight?" I yelled above the racket.

He switched off the vacuum cleaner. "Yes."

"Today is Evelyn's birthday. Her mama is doing a little party
thing for her tonight. I'm taking Saundra with me."

Hugo could read the change in my demeanor. "What's wrong?"

"Aw . . . nothing . . . just thinking about Dayton."

"That's been happening a lot lately."

"Yeah. I just keep thinking that Saundra is getting married and
they should be at the wedding."

Hugo sat down beside me. "Send them an invitation."

"Yeah. Right."

We both knew that was a terrible idea.

"I'm serious, Phil."

"And how am I supposed to explain them to Saundra?"

I had told Saundra's mother that I was an orphan and never
bothered to correct the lie with my daughter.

"You're caught in a web of lies, Phil," Hugo said gently. "I'm really sorry for you, my friend."

"Maybe telling Saundra about my family is the way to start
when I finally tell her the secret."

Hugo's dark eyes filled with sadness. "You wonder if she'll feel
sorry enough for you about the family thing that she will forgive
the rest. Guess what, old buddy? She won't."

I swept the cards off the table and sank back against the pillows.

Chapter 25

EVELYN

Saundra and I have a great relationship. Hugo says that I've modeled her in my own image but, if that is true, I didn't do it deliberately. She was searching for a mother figure when we met. All I did was just be myself. Share my views with her. I'm genuinely flattered that she liked me enough to embrace a holistic lifestyle for herself. I guess Saundra has become the daughter that I will never have. Somewhere after the misery of my own first pregnancy, I decided that I would never try again. Not because I don't like small children. It's probably because I joined the police force. Even though female officers rarely get killed in the line of duty, why take the chance on leaving an orphan behind for my mother to care for?

It's interesting that Phil hasn't changed one bit since the day we met. He never stopped eating meat. Never stopped drinking. Never got into yoga. Never started meditating, and has absolutely no patience with what he calls "new age nonsense." But what would have been the point of leaving him? It's not like there is a surplus of African-American men who don't mind being in a relationship with a woman who carries a pistol and studies Eastern philosophy.

I've often wondered why he has stayed with me for so long but that is not a smart question to ask a mate. I just chalk it all up to "opposites attract" and enjoy the time we spend together.

Sex is the only area of our relationship where Phil was totally open to my viewpoint. Sex and money cause most of the world's problems and I had to be totally honest about how firmly I believe this. When we first met, I told him that sex should not be the glue that holds a relationship together. He agreed with me that we should abstain from intercourse with each other for months at a time to make sure that we genuinely loved, respected, and cherished each other as human beings.

Sometimes, he takes the abstaining from sex thing too far. Tonight is an example. There are certain days of the year that no woman should have to ask for what she needs. It is my birthday but he is bringing Saundra with him to the celebration. What he should do is leave her back at the house with Yero, then spend time with my family and friends and whisk me out of here to a nice hotel right after I blow out the candles on my birthday cake. I mean, come on!

When Phil and Saundra pulled up in the driveway, my little party was in full swing. Mama had decorated our little home in purple. Purple crepe paper streamers. Purple balloons. A purple piñata. Purple party hats. Purple plates and cups. Even purple noisemakers. Josephine, her husband Charles and their two boys had joined us along with Mama's "friend" Tim from the butcher shop. We were eating pasta, sipping apple juice and moving our bodies to the music from a jazz CD.

Mama opened the front door and Phil lifted her right off the floor and swung her around. She playfully swatted him on his big bear chest and demanded to be put down. He and Saundra were bearing gifts. Boxes decorated in purple paper.

Phil looked a little sad and I made a mental note to question him about it some other time. He definitely worked too hard and I'd be happy when Saundra's wedding was over so he wouldn't have to pull so many double shifts. Saundra, as always, was sweet and cheerful.

Phil sat down beside me and whispered, "Happy birthday,

sweetheart," into my ear as the others laughed and joked with each other.

I squeezed his hand. "Thanks. Are you hungry?"

"Starved."

In the kitchen, I was fixing him a plate of food when I heard Phil mention the retreat.

Charles voice was loud and firm. "These women of ours just can't be satisfied with what they have."

Phil started laughing. "Oh, don't sweat it, man. They're going to do a great job. In fact, we men should be grateful. Women go up to their place, chill out and come home happy. No attitudes. No slammed doors. I tell you, it's a blessing."

"Come on, brother! How long do you think this thing will last?"

I made a plate for Saundra, too.

"It'll be a huge success!"

Charles sounded annoyed. "Well, maybe Evelyn has money to burn but I certainly don't. I told Josephine last night that she's going to have to put this dream on the back burner for a while."

He what? And when was Josephine planning to tell me?

I put a smile on my face and swept back into the living room, handing out plates like I was dispensing gold bars.

Josephine avoided my eyes and, for the next hour, I had to party like nothing was wrong. Finally, it was time for the Happy Birthday song. Then I took a deep breath, wished for inner peace, and blew out every candle on the first try.

Chapter 26

ASHA

I had never wanted a dog in the first place so Peaches had to go. I dropped him off at the dog pound one morning on my way to work and promptly erased him from my brain.

Just when Randy finally stopped calling me, I had to call him. I forgot that I lent him my mother's prized autographed copy of Miles Davis's *Kind Of Blue* album.

Saundra would have never forgiven me for losing it.

It was a nerve-popping day at the office because many executives were out and that meant more work for everyone else. My mood was so pissy when I came home that I had to drink a cocktail before calling to track down the album.

When I finally picked up the receiver to dial Randy, I took a deep breath and then forced myself to punch the numbers. With every ring of his phone, my nerves felt tighter and tighter.

"Yes?" A woman's voice answered softly.

Oh, Mr. Randy sure recovered fast. But then again, he probably had this chick on the side the whole time.

"May I speak to Randy Thompson please?" I said, trying to sound like it was a business call. She paused for a long time. *Uh-oh* I thought to myself; she's probably going to start that "my man" shit.

"I'm sorry to tell you this but Randy died yesterday," she said with increasing emotion.

"Excuse me?" I asked, not believing what I heard.

"Randy was found in his apartment by the landlord."

My heartbeat had gradually increased in speed and now it was thundering relentlessly in my chest. My mouth was drying up and I knew I had to say something before all the moisture disappeared.

"How . . . What . . . Oh, my God," I stuttered putting my hand over my mouth.

"His neighbor said Randy had his music blaring and he called the landlord to complain. Randy *never* played his music that loud and then . . ."

The woman began to cry and I had a lump in my throat the size of an apple. The shock of this news left me temporarily mute and I waited helplessly for her to finish her story.

"He had a heart attack. He was found slumped over on the toilet with liquor bottles everywhere. My poor cousin," she said, breaking down into a long sob.

The phone felt like a barbell in my hand and I struggled desperately to keep the weight near my ear. The weakness in my upper body quickly spread like a virus to my legs and I knew if I tried to stand I'd buckle like a newborn fawn. I parted my dry lips in an attempt to speak.

"Oh . . . noooo."

"I can't believe it either; he had everything going for himself. Are you a friend of his?" she asked, sniveling after every word.

"Yes, I . . . I . . . just can't . . ." I mumbled.

"I know, dear; it's a hard time for all of us; but the Lord will pull us through. Let me have your name and number so that I can inform you of the funeral arrangements. By the way, I'm his cousin Dorothy Jenkins. I will be arranging everything because his mother is overcome with grief."

When she mentioned a funeral, my body froze and I felt a chill run down my spine.

"Nice to meet you ma'am. . . ."

"Ma'am? I'm not that old, sweetie," she said with a weak chuckle.

I could do nothing but stare into space.

"My name is Saundra Patterson," I lied, trying to sound calm.

I gave her Saundra's address and phone number.

"OK dear. I'll be in touch."

"Thank you and . . . I'm sorry . . ." I trailed.

"We all are, dear, we all are. Take care." She sighed.

"Bye-bye," I whispered and hung up.

This was so unreal. I felt like a grief-stricken damsel in a made-for-TV movie. My thoughts went around in circles.

Why would Randy's heart just give out? It's all my fault. Maybe if I would have let him go a little easier he wouldn't be . . . I can't say it. He should have just found someone else. They usually do. Oh, gosh, I gotta call Saundra first thing in the morning and tell her before that lady calls her.

I figured that Randy had told everyone that I dumped him. I just *couldn't* tell that lady my real name because I didn't want any angry family members to kick my ass.

His big-ass sister, Velma, was 300 pounds of black woman that I didn't want to deal with.

The next morning it was hard to get out of bed. I decided to take the next couple of days off to clear my head and deal with this. It didn't matter anyway because my boss was somewhere tanning in St. Croix with his mistress. I know because we took the same "business trip" a couple of years ago. Yes, he would scream at me since our department was so short-staffed, but I'd deal with that when it happened.

Saundra's phone rang repeatedly and I was just about to give up when someone picked up.

"Peace," a male voice answered groggily.

"Hey, Yero. Is Saundra there?"

"Hold on," he said with a tinge of annoyance. I heard Saundra clearing her throat.

"Hello?" she asked with a crack in her voice.

"It's me, girl. I have something to tell you," I said.

"What's the matter?"

"You're not going to believe this but . . ."

"Yeah . . ."

"Randy had a heart attack," I said, feeling weak again.

"That's not funny, Asha," she said, sounding angry.

"I'm not joking, Saundra. Randy is dead."

"You serious?"

"I can't believe it either. His cousin told me . . . and it's all my fault," I said with tears welling up in my eyes.

Saundra was silent and I felt ten times worse that she didn't dispute my last remark. As the water continued to flow down my cheeks, I could sense that Saundra's silence showed her immense sadness and disgust for me.

"Asha, this is terrible, but I knew one day something like this was going to happen. You use people until you're satisfied and then dump them like trash. It was just a matter of time before disaster struck."

"I didn't mean to hurt anyone," I said, wiping my nose with a tissue.

"So closing the door in someone's face after they tell you they love you is not painful. I see," she scoffed.

I shut my eyes tight and frowned from the pain of hearing my crime.

Saundra sucked her teeth and sighed heavily. "All I have to say is that if you don't change your ways *now*, I don't want to deal with you anymore because that shows you have no heart at all. Randy's death is definitely a message for you to reevaluate yourself and clean the worms out of the pot that is your shallow little mind."

Normally I wouldn't have taken that kind of abuse but I felt it was necessary; I deserved every bit of her tongue-lashing. My chest was heaving and I could hardly breathe because of the mucus in my throat.

"I know," I said softly.

"Now that we're on the subject, I think you need to come to terms with why you began acting like this in the first place. After your pregnancy and Dante's reaction, you became a monster. I understand that it was painful but you don't have to make others suffer because you have issues. You were such a fun and happy person before all that happened. Sometimes I see a glimpse of who you were, but it's not too long before that selfish, ego-tripping thing reemerges."

When she mentioned Dante's name all I could do was remember the pain I felt on the abortion table and I started to cry again.

"Asha, I'm sorry for being so harsh but it's true, you let a bad experience at sixteen dictate the last eight years of your life. I think you've given Dante way too much of your energy. All the guys you used and hurt were symbols of him and now it's time to free yourself," she said in a more soothing tone.

As the pictures of all the men I'd taken advantage of over the years flashed in front of me, all I could do was shake my head in disbelief and remorse. I hated Saundra at that moment because, just like most people, I don't like to sniff my own shit.

"Saundra, I really don't know what to say."

"Say that you acknowledge what I'm saying to you and *change*," she stressed.

"I don't know if I can change; I am who I am. Life made me what I am."

"You *can* change, and don't give me any excuses because there are none. Just do what you gotta do," she said.

"I'll try my best."

"You don't have to make me any promises, Asha, because you're only hurting yourself," Saundra said softly.

I nodded as if she could see me, and rubbed my irritated eyes.

"Where did he die, anyway?" she asked.

"He was found on the toilet. His cousin said there were liquor bottles everywhere."

"Mmm. What a lonely way to die. Drunk and having chest pains in the john," she mumbled.

I quickly decided to hurry the conversation along because I knew if she continued to speak about how lonely he was, I'd cry again.

"I gave his cousin Dorothy your phone number so she can let you know when the funeral is. I hope you don't mind."

"It doesn't matter now, anyway, but why'd you give her my number?"

"Because I don't want to get an ass-kicking from his sister and I know he told them what I did to him."

"True; I'm sure from what you told me about his sister, she'd do it well." She chuckled.

I didn't think that was funny at all. "I have to go shopping for a black dress. I have one already but it's a bit inappropriate for the occasion."

"Hold up. I *know* you're not planning on going to the funeral? Didn't you just say you *don't* want an ass-whipping?" she asked with disbelief.

"Of course I wouldn't go as *myself*; I'd wear a disguise."

"You are such a drama queen!"

With every passing second, purchasing a red wig and Mr. Magoo glasses seemed more and more ridiculous. "Maybe you're right; I'll just remember Randy as he was."

"Yes, please do," she said sarcastically.

"Let me know when Dorothy calls."

Dorothy called Saundra on Friday to let her know that the funeral was going to be held on Saturday at eleven o'clock at the Walter B. Cook funeral home on 72nd Street. My weekend was horrible because I kept having nightmares about Randy coming towards me, gasping and holding his chest. The only way to make these nightmares stop was to face the coffin and say good-bye.

I put on the only black dress I owned and wore a blazer over it to cover the plunging neckline.

As my cab pulled up near the funeral home, I peered cautiously out of the window. Seventy-second Street was lined up with shiny black Town Cars and I didn't want anyone to see me. When I got out of the car I noticed a fat white guy getting out of a red car in front of me blowing his nose into a handkerchief. I realized he was one of Randy's coworkers whom I saw him with the night we met at B Smith's.

Bowing my head, I tied a black scarf around my face and put

on my sunglasses. Walking down the long tree-lined block, I spotted the hearse. It sat there cold and unmoving and looked like eternity itself. It troubled me to look directly at it and I strained to look at everything around it, but I couldn't. It was massive, with all of its silver swirling metal and wine-colored drapes. I began to tremble and my sunglasses began to fog up from the heat I was generating. An old frail black man stood at the door of the funeral home, wearing a tuxedo, white gloves and a stoic look on his face.

This scene of misery contradicted the happy twinkling lights and merry images of Santa that were on display on every building nearby.

My feet seemed to be cemented to the pavement and my immobility was frustrating me by the second.

Two men with the same look as the old man appeared and went over to the hearse.

Oh, my God! I thought to myself, *they're going to take him out.* My heart began to race and every muscle inside my body went into shock with the sudden rush of adrenaline.

As the head of the mahogany casket appeared, tears showered my face and I was forced to remove my eyewear.

I heard Ms. Thompson scream, "NO! NOT MY BABY, OH, GOD, NOOO!" as she stepped out of a limousine, and it was more than I could stand.

Without thinking I took off down the block and hailed a cab.

I sank deeper and deeper into depression and I couldn't seem to shake it. To make matters worse, Randy's sister kept calling, threatening to kill me.

Saundra said I was a fool for not calling the police but my guilt prevented me from lifting so much as a finger in my own defense. As if I wasn't suffering enough already, Velma sent me a copy of his love letter to me. It was dated the morning he died.

I thought about how pleased he was with his little family on Thanksgiving and how proud his mother's eyes looked whenever her son uttered but a mere sound at the dinner table. Now, because of me, there would be no more cherished moments like those; and the images of an empty seat at their old wooden table made my heart heavy and my eyes water.

When I returned to work, I was flooded with condolence cards, flowers, stale chocolates and lunch invitations, but it was Saundra who snapped me out of my doldrums.

I invited her over for dinner and bought some appetizers from her favorite restaurant to go along with the meal.

She arrived at my house about six-thirty and when she saw the trademark transparent bag from Zen Palate on the kitchen table, she gave me the warmest hug she could muster. Saundra is truly an amazing person; she appreciates the littlest things people do for her as if they were so much more.

"Are you feeling better at all, Asha?" she asked as she flopped down on the couch with a spring roll.

"A little, I guess; every day it gets a lot easier. I would be even better if Velma would stop bugging me," I said, chopping onions in the kitchen.

"You shouldn't have spent so much time alone."

"Nick wanted to fly in but I just wasn't in the mood to entertain someone. Besides, Velma still calls from time to time. Nick would have wanted to know what all the ruckus is about."

"I don't understand why you're doing this to yourself. You should call the police and have them put a stop to this nonsense before it goes too far."

"Velma is not really going to hurt me. She's just trying to make me feel bad and she's doing a damn good job of it."

"You should stop beating yourself up over this now. True, you have made some horrible mistakes, but maybe he just had a bad heart and didn't know it."

"He would be alive if he hadn't met me," I said, tossing the onions into the hot skillet.

"I don't believe that, per se. Only God knows why He called Nick home."

Maybe Saundra's visit was just what the doctor ordered.

"Thanks, Saundra, I really needed to hear that," I said, breathing a sigh of relief.

"It's true. Now will you try to cheer up?" she asked with her mouth half full.

And just like that, I was all better. Randy was a thing of the past. However, I kept my sad expression in place so Saundra wouldn't call me callous again. "I'll try."

"That's all I ask," she said, putting her plate in the sink.

For the next couple of hours we had a ball watching Saundra's favorite kung-fu movies with terrible voice-overs and no plots. I hadn't watched them since I was a child and it bought back many wonderful memories of Mama, who'd enjoyed them, too.

Afterwards we played "dress up" like little girls and fell out on each other as we exchanged clothes.

At about eleven o'clock we decided to wind things down and played some of Mom's favorite music from the seventies. Curtis Mayfield chilled things out perfectly with his silky voice and soft pulse. It had been a long time since I had a fun Saturday.

"I'm so happy you came over Saundra; you've really cheered me up," I said, folding out the couch bed.

"I'm glad to hear that, after you avoided me like the plague," she said, laughing.

"I'm sorry about that, but I just had so much on my mind and I really needed to be alone and sort some things out," I explained.

"I understand that but the least you could've done is told me that, not just drop off the face of the earth," she said, looking at me seriously.

"Sorry about that," I said again.

"Oh, well, it's over and done with. Can I use your phone?" she asked, walking towards my little white cell.

I began to laugh out loud and she looked at me as if I was crazy.

"And what is so funny?" she asked, putting her hands on her hips.

"You gotta check up, huh?" I said with the grin still spread across my face.

She laughed and waved her hand at me. "How do you know I'm going to call Yero?"

"Yero? I didn't say nothin' about no Yero; I meant your father."

"I'm not paying you any mind," she said, turning her back to dial.

I got up and went to the bathroom and noticed Saundra's duffle bag was filled with huge sanitary napkins, the size of pillows. I laughed and grabbed one up and marched back out with it swaying freely in my hand. With a smirk on my face I walked up behind her and tapped her on the shoulder. Her head was tilted as she listened to the person on the other end and she scrunched up her nose at my intrusion. I held up the oversize maxi and we both exploded with laughter. After apologizing and cooing "I love you" to Yero she hit me playfully on the arm and hung up.

"Why did you do that?" She smiled.

"No, the question is, why do you have these big-ass pads?" I snickered, going to the bathroom to return it.

"The bigger they are, the better protection I have and I don't care if they look ugly."

"No wonder you always look like you're spawning a dick every month".

"Shut up!" She giggled.

"Are you okay? You don't have any cramps do you? Cause I have some really good pills to help," I shouted from behind the door.

"I don't have menstrual cramps most of the time and when I do, I drink herbal tea and I'm fine."

I rolled my eyes at her response because I get cramps that sometimes make it hard to walk. At that moment the most horrific thought entered my mind and I came rushing out into the room.

"What's the matter, Asha?" she said, coming to me.

The room began to spin and she helped me sit down on the edge of the bed.

"Come on, girl, speak to me!" she said, shaking me lightly on both shoulders.

"I . . . I . . . don't remember getting my . . ." I said, feeling my stomach tensing up.

Saundra's face was frozen and her thin eyebrows hung high in the air.

"What? Wait a minute. You're not saying what I think you're gonna say," she said, getting up, walking towards the window with her hand plastered to her forehead.

"I haven't gotten my period since November," I said, choking back the tears.

"Nah, this can't be happening. Was it before or after you were intimate with Nick?"

"After," I whispered in despair at the thought of being pregnant with Randy's baby.

"Oh, my God, Asha, you don't think . . . I mean, were you with anyone else besides Randy after Nick?" she asked with hope.

"No." I sighed and lay down on the bed in fetal position.

"Oh, man, this is way too much," she said, pacing across the floor with her head in her hands.

I listened to the creaking sound her feet made across the wooden floor and her heavy sighs, and I wanted to scream. I felt as if I was trapped in the *Twilight Zone* and there was nowhere to run. How could I possibly be pregnant when Randy and I always used a condom? The odds of that happening were a million to one and I had the unwelcome honor of becoming that one percent statistic. I wished that I wasn't allergic to birth control pills because I would've taken them by the handful. I jumped up from the bed like lightning and ran into the kitchen.

"Don't do anything stupid!" Saundra yelled behind me.

I picked up the fifth of rum and poured myself a teacup full and downed my shot like I was in a Western.

"Shit!" I screamed as loud as I could and slammed down the cup.

Chapter 27

SAUNDRA

Today Asha is supposed to go see a doctor during her lunch hour. I can't imagine what it must feel like to be pregnant with a deceased lover's baby, or even worse, for that child to grow up knowing its father had a heart attack because its mother was a bitch.

I still can't believe Randy died and I regret not staying on the phone a couple of more hours when he had called me, but I guess there is nothing I could have done to ease his pain. If that's not distressing enough, his sister is making Asha's life a living hell. Although I know things happen for a reason and there are no "accidents," I still wish that I could make things easier for Asha.

In a way I feel kind of bad that I kept calling her a "karma time bomb" because that's exactly what she turned out to be and, boy, did it explode. I think it's a shame when pregnancies are unplanned because I believe it has negative effects on the mother. No matter how much love is between them, the mother will always subconsciously know she didn't mean for it to happen.

I also don't understand why a woman would sleep with a man if he's not fit enough to father a child because every time you have sex pregnancy is a possibility, regardless of contraceptive devices.

Another one headed for bad karma is my dear father, Phillip. I have reasons to suspect that he is being unfaithful to Evelyn. He's been coming home late from work, chuckles all night on the phone like an adolescent and shops a lot more.

What is especially strange is that of all the bags he brings home, I never see the contents of any of them. It seems like after he buys whatever it is, it just disappears without a trace. Although I'm dying of curiosity, I wouldn't dare invade his privacy. Sometimes I think I'm just *too* good.

Yero doesn't think he's cheating on Evelyn but he did say my father might be purchasing some kinky sex toys. I laughed with repulsion at the notion and rejected it immediately. My father is a cop for crying out loud. He *busts* perverts like that.

Yero smiled in that "you never know" way and I turned my back on him.

It feels *sooo* good to finally be on vacation after last month's hectic schedule. The month's Black Heroes celebration at the community center was a disaster. Someone had broken into the center the night before and stolen everything in sight, including the children's artwork.

The children were disappointed because they had worked so hard to raise money for the celebration by selling raffle tickets and candy. Everyone's heart sank when we saw the cold empty space that once housed beautiful decorations and a warm cedar-wood kinara. As the howling children were comforted by the counselors, I wondered who could be so low as to steal from the kids.

Yero and I had planned a wonderful program filled with arts and crafts, plays, folk tales and a fashion show. Yero decided that we shouldn't let the situation ruin our holiday so he decided to have everybody over at his house. There was no point in staying at the community center because it would've been too depressing for the children and counselors alike. Since we called his mother at the last minute, we didn't have all of the trimmings but it turned out to be a joyous celebration just the same. We told the children that their heroes are in their hearts and maybe that was a better lesson for them to learn anyhow.

When I saw Yero with all of those children, doing face painting,

I couldn't help but smile. I remembered his behavior when he heard that Khari was going to make him an uncle and knew he had just lashed out in fear. He loved kids and would be a great father to our many many children.

He never talks about Khari and Joanne's situation anymore.

Joanne comes from a strict Haitian family which threw her out when she got pregnant. Not only do they not like Khari because he's American, they won't accept a sexually active unmarried daughter.

Her parents told her they want nothing to do with her even though she isn't expecting anymore. They had high hopes for her to be a lawyer, marry a Haitian man from a good family and live happily ever after. She said that the only way matters could be worse is if Khari was Jamaican.

While Yero told me all of this, I shook my head repeatedly with disgust and disbelief. What the hell difference does it make where we're from when we have other battles to confront? I remember the girls in high school fighting over the same "Island Wars" and it seemed stupid then and it still is. My father always taught me that we are all black people who may have come on different ships but are still in the same boat. I wish all black people could wake up and see that.

Right now the primary focus should be on Joanne's mental health not nationality.

I swear I will never understand parents like Jo's; how can you kick your child out like that? I could see if she was on drugs, stealing, or something like that, but I can't picture putting your pregnant daughter out. They don't even know what kind of environment she's going to be in and they never saw Khari's mother a day in their lives. Luckily for her, Denise treats her son's girlfriends like family or Jo would really be knee deep.

Sometimes other people's problems can be exhausting to listen to.

Sitting in front of my bedroom window I watched the sun descend into the horizon, causing an array of colors to blend across the fading blue palette that was day. The bright fuchsia-colored clouds quickly swept towards the west, pushed hastily by the brisk

January air. During a brief moment of drifting between thoughts, I remembered what I realized on the train to school this morning.

A homeless man came into the first car carrying a cardboard sign expressing his misfortune, a soiled old coffee cup and an unbearable stench. I just happened to be looking around at the people's reaction to him and they were all different. Some turned their heads in the other direction, some closed their eyes and pretended not to see him, some got angry that he was there, some looked at other people for someone else to share their disgust and some threw a few coins in his cup; but *none* of them actually looked the man in the eyes. The reason why I found this so interesting is because the way the people responded to the homeless man is the same way most people respond to the truth.

They just don't want to see it.

Chapter 28

ASHA

Dr. Singh is supposed to get back to me today at three o'clock with the results of my blood pregnancy test and I'm nervous as hell. At the company meeting this morning while my boss rambled, all I could think about was my distorted body draped in a long sack-like dress with an ugly floral print on it. I was horrified by the visualization and I blinked hard to squeeze it out of my mind. The suspense is killing me and I'm seriously considering running to Duane Reade's for a pregnancy test even though I don't really believe in over-the-counter diagnoses.

Patience is not one of my virtues and I can't take it anymore. I jumped up from my desk, quickly grabbed my coat from the closet and bolted out the door. When I got to the store I was annoyed by the vast selection of products, so I just grabbed the one that showed the plus or minus sign.

After squeezing a couple of drops of urine in the disk in the company bathroom, I carefully carried the gadget to my office wrapped up in some toilet tissue. I placed it on the desk and sat there staring at it. The laughter outside of my office broke my concentration and just when I was about to close the door, my supervisor walked in. I froze in place.

"Excuse me, Asha, I don't mean to disturb you but I just had to come and thank you personally for the wonderful job you did representing the company last week at the buyers' conference. Everyone said you were quite remarkable," he said, extending his hand in congratulations.

"Thank you, Mr. Delrossi, I appreciate that. How have you been?" I asked, shaking his cold clammy hand.

"I've asked you before to please call me Ralph," he said, smiling, with his hands folded.

"All right—Ralph. How is everything?" I chuckled.

"Everything is fine, thank you. My eldest son Ted just got accepted to Yale and my wife and I are very proud of him."

"You have reason to be. He's a very handsome boy." I wanted to tell Ralph that his little Yalie was boffing his assistant but it seemed like a bad idea.

"Why, thank you; good looks run in the family, you know." He winked and smiled.

I suppressed the desire to slap my knee as I looked at his big red sweaty face and sparse gray hair slicked down over a gigantic bald spot.

"May I use your phone, please?" he asked, already motioning towards the desk.

"Sure."

I was mortified as he moved the wad of tissue over to clear his way. As I turned my back so he wouldn't see what must have been a real stupid look on my face, the unimaginable happened. I heard something drop on the floor and when I turned around, I could tell by his uncomfortable expression and the sheer brightness of the new shade of crimson he had turned that it was the test. *Somebody just shoot me now* I thought as I dived on the floor for the small plastic stick. It had managed to roll underneath the desk and I was forced to tap his leg for him to move over so I could reach it. What could he possibly be thinking as I scrounged around for a pregnancy test with my ass in the air?

When I finally came back up grasping it tightly in my right hand, he was staring out the window muttering commands on the phone to his assistant but I could tell that he was just as embarrassed as I was because he was shifting from one leg to the other. Humiliated already, I decided to go ahead and look at the damn result and I was thrilled to see the tiny minus sign emblazoned in pink on the surface. I threw it in the garbage hastily and straightened out my clothes. My stockings now had a run on the left leg that went straight up to my thigh but that was irrelevant. I walked over to my fax machine and pretended to fax someone a letter but a stupid-ass computerized voice called me out by saying loudly "No receiver, no receiver!" I turned around to see if he was looking and we locked eyes briefly. As his conversation wound down I wanted the floor to open up and swallow me.

"Thank you for letting me use your phone, and I'll see you later," he said, smiling uneasily.

"Good-bye, Mr. Delrossi," I said softly.

He waved without looking back and disappeared down the corridor. I have never been so embarrassed in my life. What a fool he must think I am *and* tacky too. Well who the fuck cares. The little stick says that I'm not pregnant!!!

When I got home I saw the red light flashing on my answering machine and I couldn't believe it said I had twenty messages. Two of them were from Saundra and the rest were from that crazy bitch Velma. I have had enough of this shit and I'm not taking this anymore. This whole scenario has taken too much of my time already and I'll be damned if this ghetto heifer is going to keep me where I don't want to be. I pressed *69 to tell this stupid-ass welfare-check-gettin' ho of a sister to leave me the hell alone or I'm going to get her fat ass arrested.

"Hello?" a little voice answered.

"May I speak to Velma please?"

"Hol' on," she said, dropping the phone to the ground. I flinched from the sound of the impact. "Mama! Mama!" I heard Alize frantically calling in the background.

"What!" I heard Velma ask.

"Some white lady's on the phone, she wants to talk to you."

White lady? I thought to myself. This poor girl hardly hears proper English so she thinks I'm white. How unfortunate.

"Hello?" Velma answered, out of breath.

"This is Asha Mitchell. I really don't appreciate your leaving messages on my machine and if you don't stop harassing me, I'm going to call the police immediately," I said crisply.

"Bitch . . . I don't give a fuck what you *appreciate*. You lucky I don't put your ass right next to my brother!" she screamed.

"I'm sorry about your brother but that's not my fault. God just called him home, Velma."

"Fuck you, bitch! You don't know shit!"

"Fine. I will call the police if you continue and they will cut off your check *and* your food stamps, so do yourself a favor and stop." I said firmly.

"No you don't. You fuckin'. . . . !"

Dial tone. I think I got my point across and if I didn't, she'll be in jail on Rikers Island by sunup, no problem.

After eating a little and watching TV, I figured Saundra should be home by now. I smiled to myself as I thought about how I slammed the phone down in Velma's ear, which was probably still ringing. There are two things I have learned from watching old movies: how to slap a man and how to hang up a telephone.

"Hey, girl!"

"I'm not pregnant!" I exclaimed.

"When did you find out?"

"At work. I went to Duane Reade and got a pregnancy test."

"I thought you wanted a blood test instead of the quickie kind. What happened to the doctor?"

"He left a message on my voice mail saying the same thing."

"I'm glad to hear it, Asha."

"Well, *whatever*. I'm not a mommy and that's all that matters right now."

"What are you doing this Saturday?"

"You know that I don't do anything when I'm in between con-quests."

"Asha . . . Remember you said you were going to try to change that, right? There're not going to *be* anymore conquests, right?" she said, dragging her words.

"Yeah, yeah . . . Why do you ask?"

"I want you to come to a tea party with me in Brooklyn," she said happily.

"I heard you talking about those tea parties a while ago. Isn't that where a bunch of you new age, '70s rejects get together and complain about The Man?" I giggled.

"Ha, ha, very funny; but it's really not like that. We discuss a lot of different things and people, and also read their creative work; you'll get to meet a lot of nice people and besides, its better than sitting in the house all weekend"

"I don't know, Saundra, you know I'm not into all that stuff."

"Well, let me know if you change your mind but I think you'd enjoy yourself."

"Anyway, guess what just happened right before I called you?" I said, changing the topic on purpose.

"What?"

"I finally got the balls to call Velma and tell her off."

"Did the sun pass the moon or something? What made you do *that* after all this time?" she asked.

"When I got home, there were eighteen messages from her and I just got fed up."

"What did you say when you called?"

"I told her I'd have her arrested and the police would take her welfare and food stamps away!" I laughed.

"Oh, no, you didn't say *that*! Are you serious?" She cackled.

"Hell, yeah! And then she got all shanehneh on me and shit! She kept saying, oh, no, you don't," I said, imitating Martin Lawrence.

"You are really too much but I have to go take a shower now because I'm going out with Yero in a half hour and the least I can do is not be funky."

"All right, I'll catch you later."

"Peace," she said and hung up.

Maybe I should go out with Saundra this weekend. I haven't been out in a long time and she doesn't ask much of me. Besides, I need to escape.

They are definitely on CP time. Saundra said they would be here to pick me up by one and it's already two thirty-nine. In the meantime I decided to get some work done. Of course, as soon as

I decided to do something else that's when they showed up. Saundra yelled up to my window and I quickly ran downstairs to prevent any complaints from my neighbors. When she saw what I was wearing, her eyebrows shot up.

"That dashiki is *off the meter.* Where'd you get it?" she asked staring at its swirling patterns.

"I just bought it yesterday when I decided to come with you."

"That looks really good; you look beautiful," she said, giving me a hug.

"Well, you know what they say, when in Rome . . ."

She rolled her eyes and walked towards the car. I couldn't believe I was actually getting in this big lime green car to go to some damn tea party. Boy, did Randy screw my head up.

Yero and I exchanged greetings and I couldn't help rolling my eyes. I will never marry a poor man. Ever.

Saundra glared at me and then turned around to introduce me to the two people in the backseat.

"This is my friend Kimiko, the one I'm always telling you about from school, and this is Jazz, she's going to be reading tonight."

"Hi, nice to meet you," I said, extending my hand to both of them. Yero started the car and then he reached into the glove compartment to get a tape. I prayed for no sounds of nature or *whatever* shit they listen to. As he pulled away from the curb, Erykah Badu filled the car and I was relieved, I can handle *her.*

The one thing that puzzles me is Saundra's friend Kimiko. She is Asian but she was wearing a headwrap. If it's all about being yourself and all that, why the hell isn't she wearing a kimono or something? Why a headwrap? I'll ask Saundra later when I get her alone because I can't figure that out for the life of me. I didn't speak much on the way there because I always like to know who I'm dealing with, but I would periodically laugh at some of the funny stuff they said. Jazz was the one who had everyone in stitches because she's so blatant about everything she feels. Kimiko was extremely laid back but would put her two cents in when she felt it was necessary. I thought they would all be in here talking about the ozone layer or whatever but they were acting so silly, I actually found myself laughing. Maybe I *won't* be in tears for Mother Earth by the end of the evening.

The tea party place was cool, dimly lit and extremely mellow. There was one amateurishly set up spotlight that tilted slightly to the left but the sound system was on point. The music wasn't too soft or too loud but just hung there in the background for those who wanted to pay attention.

There was a mix of ethnic groups. Latinos, Asians, and Indians from the East and West. Everyone seemed so comfortable with each other and I now understood why Kimiko looked the way she did. There were no chairs, just big pillows for people to sit on.

While Saundra and the rest of her entourage excused themselves to greet their friends, I sat there truly mesmerized by the beautiful artworks strategically placed along the walls. One in particular caught my eye. It was a painting of a black woman as the bark of a tree, her legs becoming one with the soil, limbs for arms, and colorful autumn leaves for hair. She was one of many trees in the forest but the farther the other trees were away from her, the more decayed they became. Her eyes were closed and her face had a look of peace and tranquillity on it as if she wasn't concerned with dying or blossoming, she simply was going along with the cycle of life. The mixture of techniques and different paints such as acrylic and oil gave her such a rich texture that she looked carved and seemed to pop off the canvas. The artist was truly a master at the placement of color, recreating the feeling of dawn. Indigo, violet, scarlet and saffron lighting came peeking through the leaves, illuminating her surroundings.

Saundra materialized at my side. "So, what do you think? Not so bad, right?"

"No, it's cool, but don't get too excited," I warned her. "I'm not ready to live in your world full time."

She sucked her teeth and sat down next to me on the huge orange pillow. "There are so many people who I want you to meet but I think we're about to start so I don't want to get the social train steaming just yet," she said, pulling a bottled water out of her bag.

"That's fine . . . but . . . uh, do you know the person who did that painting up there, it's *bad*," I said, lifting my head up.

"I know, it's one of the best pieces in here. It's called "Is." My friend Derrick did that," she said proudly.

"He really has a lot of talent. Is he going to be here tonight?"

"I'm not sure, let me ask Yero," she said, tapping him on the shoulder.

Yero was in a huddle with Kimiko and Jazz.

"Excuse me, baby, but do you know if Derrick will be here tonight?"

"He said he's reading today so he should be here any minute," he said quickly, turning back around.

She looked at me and started grinning and I tried my best to have an innocent look in my eyes.

"Why are you so interested in meeting Derrick?" Saundra asked, passing me an orange out of her bag.

I began to peel the orange and avoided eye contact to hide my excitement. "I just think his work is phenomenal and I want to put a face with the painting; you know how much I like the finer things in life," I said, biting into the juicy orange.

"If you like that one, wait till you see his portfolio," she said with her eyes wide.

"What does he look like?" I asked, hoping he wasn't dog-ass ugly.

"He's definitely not *your* type, he's not all *GQ* or whatever." She shrugged.

"I *asked* you what he looked like, not for a synopsis of my taste."

"He's very tall, slender, long locks, brown skinned . . . *I* think he's gorgeous."

"How does he dress?" I asked, not impressed so far.

"He usually wears jeans, cargo pants, T-shirts . . . very casual; but I've never seen him in a situation where that's not appropriate," she said.

He definitely doesn't sound like my type of guy because I'm not crazy about locks or the casual look, either. Oh, well, so much for *that,* but I still want to meet him anyway to discuss a possible business proposition. With his talent and my beauty, I'm sure he can do a masterpiece of me to hang up in my apartment. The walls in my apartment are way too bare, anyway, and I've always wanted a portrait of myself.

The lights began to flicker and Jazz quickly ran "backstage," which was simply a black curtain separating the huge floor space and the bedrooms. Saundra said it was about to start in five minutes and everyone began to settle down.

Yero held Saundra and I saw an Asian guy with an afro sitting down next to Kimiko; I tried not to stare.

"Asha, this is my boyfriend Lenny," Kimiko said.

Lenny smiled and extended his hand. "How you doin'?" he said, sounding Black.

"Fine, thank you," I said, not knowing what else to say.

"A'ight"

"How long have you two been dating?" I asked, feeling insipid.

"About a year now, right, boo?" Kimiko said, stroking the hair underneath his chin.

He smiled again and reached over and smacked Saundra on the top of her head. Yero turned around in defense and then eased when he saw Lenny's broad grin. Saundra gave him a pound.

"Where you been, bugger?" Saundra asked, putting her locks in a ponytail.

"Workin', school, you know the deal," he replied.

"Yeah, I know; where's your sister, she comin'?"

"Nah, she couldn't find anybody to keep Toshio so she just stayed home."

"But she could have brought Toshi with her; no one cares," Saundra said, sounding disappointed.

"I told her that but she said she hates when other people bring noisy children because it kills the effect."

"Tell her to call me."

He nodded obediently and turned to Jazz who was standing in front of the microphone silently, looking at everyone.

Jazz cleared her throat to get everyone to focus their attention on her. "May I have your attention please; we're about to begin, and out of respect for the artists, will everyone please keep down the background noise. If you must speak, please whisper softly. And if you have children, please keep them quiet or excuse yourself. Thank you."

"Saundra, are you going to perform today?" I asked, hunching over to see her face.

"Nah, I haven't written at all lately because it hasn't been raining and that's when I do my best work. Yero will be doing some stand-up comedy, though."

"I didn't know you were a comedian, Yero!" I laughed, trying to keep my voice down.

He shrugged modestly. "Not really. Sometimes me and Jazz do these little skits about stuff people can relate to, that's about it; but art is my first love."

"Yero made the sculpture that is next to the bathroom. We'll go see it during the intermission," Saundra said, smacking on some peanuts.

"I feel so ordinary amongst all of you artists," I said.

"Oh, please, don't even try it. The way you put together your clothes, what the hell do you think you are?" Saundra asked.

"Well, if that makes me an artist, then I'm fucking Picasso because I can dress my ass off!" I laughed.

Jazz interrupted what would have been one of my moments when she tapped the microphone, causing a screeching sound.

"Sorry . . . we're *really* going to start now. Is everybody ready?" she asked, trying to get everyone pumped.

"Get on with it, " a voice bellowed out, causing a sea of laughter.

Jazz stuck her tongue out at the guy and continued. "You all know him so he needs no real introduction. Here's Derrick!" she yelled, pointing to her left and clapping as she went to sit down.

After clapping for a while, everyone got super quiet and I knew that he must be really deep or something because it takes a lot for Black folks to shut up. When he came from behind the curtain some people whistled. He was *very* attractive with a beautiful set of dimples that really got me going. He had on a nice ribbed cream-colored sweater and slacks of the same color and dark brown boots. Saundra's description didn't begin to capture his gorgeousness. After smiling and waving at the people he knew for a couple of seconds he finally pulled out a crumpled up piece of loose-leaf out of his pocket. Saundra turned around and snickered because she caught me with my mouth open as he cleared his throat to read a poem he called "Plants in the Sidewalk." I ignored her childish display and listened closely to his soliloquy about truth springing up in places seemingly incapable of sustaining growth. Although I didn't understand some of the terminology that other people strongly responded to, the detailed descriptions and his emotion moved me as he read. I saw Saundra wipe her eyes a couple of times and Yero's even looked a little glassy. I noticed Kimiko and Lenny got romantic vibes from it because they were locked in a solid embrace.

As I watched Derrick leave the "stage" with a trail of tears and praise following him faithfully, I knew I was going to fuck him.

Chapter 29

SAUNDRA

Asha bugged me until I gave her Derrick's phone number and that led to a major fight between me and Yero.

"My sister is going after Derrick."

Yero chuckled. "Derrick could use a night with a hot piece like her. He is way too wrapped up in his work."

We were sitting in my favorite Indian restaurant down in Greenwich Village. As I told Daddy, the plan was to have dinner there and then spend the night together at a nearby Howard Johnson's motel just for a change of scenery. When I asked Daddy how he planned to spend his night off, he shrugged and said maybe he'd go see a movie with Evelyn.

I'd just stuffed a piece of naan into my mouth when Yero made his crude remark.

"Excuse me?" I asked politely.

"Don't get me wrong. I'm not criticizing Derrick or anything. He's going to make it as a poet someday and there's not a brother I can think of who deserves it more."

"I've never heard you talk about any woman like that, Yero, and it doesn't work for me. Especially since the woman is my sister."

"You're going to be my wife soon," Yero replied. "I should be able to speak my mind."

"Since when is your mind into denigrating women?"

Yero took my hand and massaged it. "Let's not do this."

But I couldn't let it go. "I know you don't like Asha but . . ."

"Asha doesn't like Asha."

"What?"

"I don't have any feelings about your sister one way or the other. So, you're wrong. I don't dislike her. But if Asha liked herself, she wouldn't be hitting the sheets with every man that crosses her path."

"Do me a favor, Yero?"

"What?"

"Cut the dime-store psychology. You don't know Asha at all."

"I know that if Derrick liked black women, he could hit it within an hour of meeting her."

That did it. I stood up and mushed him in the face with a large piece of naan. The hard Indian bread crumpled into his eyebrows and moustache.

Yero glared at me. I glared back.

"In the future, don't ever put your hands on me. I'm serious, Saundra. Don't ever hit me again."

He was right. It was no way to start a marriage. "I'm sorry, baby."

He grunted.

I reached forward to brush off the naan and he pushed my hand away. "Let's go," he said testily.

"But we haven't had a meal yet," I protested.

Yero narrowed his eyes. "I don't know what your problem is today but if you want a husband, you're playing the wrong game now."

I'd had it with his attitude. "Is that a threat, Yero? Are you threatening not to marry me?"

"No . . . I'm just saying watch your hands."

What game was he talking about? What did he mean . . . the wrong game? When was I ever playing ANY game? Did he think I was one of those pathetic women who played stupid games with stupid rules just to get an engagement ring placed on the third finger of their left hand? "Yero, I don't care if I never get married at all—to you or anyone else."

"Thanks a lot," he replied bitterly.

He looked hurt and all of a sudden I wasn't mad anymore; but he stood up and threw his napkin on the table before I could say the words that always worked magic between us.

"Saundra, I grew up watching my parents hit each other."

If I had hugged and kissed him at that exact moment, maybe things would have turned out differently. We would have made it to the motel and the events that took place later that terrible night would not have happened. But I'd never heard this story about Yero's parents before and that fact plus the anger in his voice just threw me off course.

So I just stood there saying nothing.

"I can't believe that you physically attacked me, Saundra."

"Yero, look . . ."

"You know what . . . I don't feel in a motel mood anymore. Let's just go."

Yes, I was wrong to hit, but when he decided to end our evening, I got mad. "Fine, Yero!"

We didn't speak to each other on the way home.

When he pulled up in front of my house, I jumped out of the car. As he drove off, I started to calm down. After all, the fight was my fault. Asha did behave like a hot piece and there was no point in me losing my man over her loose life. Should I call Yero right away or give him time to cool off? I'd ask Daddy. His car was in the driveway and Evelyn's was not, so that meant he was alone.

I took the stairs two at a time.

His bedroom door was wide open and the light was on. I skidded to a stop in front of the door and froze.

"Don't stop!" Hugo cried out, gasping for breath. "Don't come yet!"

"Move it, baby," Daddy answered passionately as he rode Hugo's naked white ass.

Hugo burrowed his face deeper into bedding and clutched a pillow with both hands. "Umm."

Daddy saw me first.

My feet were rooted to the floor as my brain tried to process the scene before me.

"Saundra! Oh, Jesus! Saundra!" Daddy finally yelped.

The sound of his voice snapped me out of my trance. "What the fuck is going on here!" I screamed.

Hugo started pulling the bedding around them as Daddy just stared at me in shock.

The Indian bread rushed up from my stomach and seemed to lodge in my throat. I started to gag.

"Saundra! I can explain!"

In one huge gush, I threw up all over the floor. Then, screaming, I started walking backwards.

"Saundra, come back!" Daddy begged, "Where are you going?"

I turned and ran down the stairs and straight to my room without answering. I grabbed a shopping bag that was on the floor and hastily flung some clothes inside.

Daddy was standing at the bottom of the stairs when I came out. "Saundra, can we talk? I can explain everything."

I raced past him, out the front door and ran across the lawn to our closest neighbor.

"Pastor Hoffman!" I screamed. "Pastor Hoffman!"

I was relieved when the elderly preacher opened his door. "Saundra, are you all right?" His eyes were wide with alarm.

"Can I come in and call a cab?"

He just stared at me and the shopping bag.

"Please?"

He peered past me, looking toward my house. "Has something happened to Detective Patterson? What is going on?"

"My father is fine. Can I come in?"

"Sure, honey."

The door closed behind me. I had little to no time before Daddy came banging on that door. "I can't stay at home tonight . . . please . . . it's personal . . ."

Pastor Hoffman held up a hand. "I don't like this Saundra. This ain't like you at all. I'll drive you wherever it is you're going."

Goddammit, I didn't have time to argue with him. "I'm going to my sister's house in Manhattan. Just call me a cab. I'll be fine."

"Where is your Daddy?"

Something inside me just snapped. "With all due respect,

Pastor Hoffman, I am a grown woman. My father is at home and I'm leaving. Now, will you help me or not?"

We sat there in his living room in silence for almost ten minutes until the taxi arrived. I ran out the door and jumped in the backseat without taking the time to say a decent good-bye.

Daddy was heading towards the vehicle.

"Drive fast!" I yelled. "That man is trying to stop me from leaving!"

The driver burned rubber pulling away from the curb, leaving Daddy standing there frantically calling my name and waving his arms.

"Take me to Manhattan . . . Sixth Avenue and Fourteenth Street." That one sentence took all the strength I had left. I curled up in a ball on the backseat and let the tears run down my face.

Chapter 30

ASHA

I got to work one morning and was surprised to find a Post-It note on my computer screen that said I should call Nick Seabrook right away.

I put my coat on the hook in the back of my office door and buzzed my assistant. "Kevin, could you come here for a moment?"

My short, red-haired assistant came in with a notepad in his hands. He is the most inefficient member of the buying office support staff, and the only reason I don't fire him is because he has a B.A. from Harvard and an M.A. from Yale. It gives me a certain amount of pleasure that someone with so much education has to take orders from me.

"Good morning, Kevin. This morning is going to be hectic so call Nick Seabrook back and tell him to try me at home tonight. Then reschedule my appointment with Lew Weimann from Zippy Girl handbags. After that, you can start letting the sales reps in."

I booted up my computer and started responding to some e-mails and was totally engrossed in the task when Kevin buzzed.

"Asha, Nick is on the phone" he said.

"Kevin, I told you that I can't talk to him now."

I answered another e-mail before he rang again. "Mr. Seabrook insists that you talk to him now. He says it will only take a minute."

"Yeah, all right put him through."

I waited for Nick's high-pitched voice to say hello but all I heard was Biggie Smalls's song "Hypnotize" blasting from his car radio.

When did Nick start listening to rap music?

"Hello?"

"Hey, girl!"

"What's up, Nick, how are you?"

"Chillin', chillin', wassup wit you?"

"Why are you speaking that way?"

"What are you doing right now?"

"Since I don't have two rich parents like you do, I'm working for a living."

"No, but you have a rich boyfriend."

Boyfriend? Both Nick and I were aware that we both dated other people. In fact, he had some lovelorn chick down in Houston. Boyfriend? For some reason, I liked the sound. Maybe because it was coming from him and not some other guy.

"True, you are pretty rich, Mr. Seabrook."

"Aiiight."

"Nick, that fake gangsta thug dialect sounds ridiculous. What are you up to?"

"I'm mentoring this teenaged brother down in Houston. It's a program for young males at risk. This is the way he communicates with me. So I'm practicing."

"Well, cut it out for right now."

"Asha, baby! Loosen up."

"I don't want to hear that kind of talk. Besides, isn't the point of him getting together with you to learn how to speak proper English?"

"No. That isn't the point at all. Now, I need your cooperation, Miss Mitchell. I'm in the middle of a twenty-four hour experiment and I have twelve hours to go."

"You're going to talk like that for the next twelve hours?"

Nick was such a spoiled rich brat. Only someone with a huge trust fund could afford to speak like a thug just for the fun of it.

"Then I feel sorry for Baby Girl."

Baby Girl was the nickname of his Houston babe.

"You're going to regret that statement in half a second."

"Nick, I'm pretty busy. What do you have to tell me that couldn't wait until tonight?"

"Well, Ms. Thang, I was callin' to tell you that you will be blessed with my company soon."

I tried to contain my excitement. "Last I heard, you were staying in Houston for another month."

"Plans change, girl. I'm home. How about I hang out at your apartment till you get there?"

"Why?"

"Because my place is in an uproar. I'm having a wall taken out to make the living room bigger."

"Yeah, all right, I'll leave my keys with Kevin but make sure you don't throw no gangsta parties while I'm at work."

"Whatever. And tell that bitch-ass secretary of yours he betta know how to talk to me. I'm about two minutes off whoopin' his carrot-top lookin' ass."

I decided to play along and talk like a round-the-way girl. Hmm, maybe we could do some kind of rap role play before hitting the sheets tonight. "Kevin looks like he might bust a cap in yo' ass."

"I'm too rich to fight. I'll just pay another muthafucka to argue for me."

He hadn't been on the phone five minutes and I was already in stitches. "You are so crazy, Nick. I'll catch you later."

"There better be more than bologna and cheese in that muthafuckin' kitchen."

God he sounded stupid but I couldn't suppress a giggle. No one can ever say that Nick is dull.

"You know I don't cook. Why didn't you bring some food from your mama's restaurant?"

"You know I don't eat no soul food. That's all they fed me growin' up."

"All right; we'll go get something different tonight when I get in."

"Cool, just make sure you get home on time."

"Yes, dear."

"Hey, Asha . . ."

"Yeah?"

"I missed you, girl."

"All right, Nick. I'll see you tonight."

I could hear the rap music blasting from my apartment. The bass line was so strong I could feel it vibrating in my chest. As soon as I walked through the door I found Nick dancing in the center of the living room in some funny-looking boxers with smiley faces on it. As angry as I was about the volume of the music, the image of him doing the Harlem shake half naked was hilarious.

"Nick!" I screamed.

He turned around and flashed that cute smile of his and turned the music down.

"Hey! I was just working off a big Whopper with cheese from Burger King. You look sooo good, girl; come here."

I put down my bag and hugged him. His arms felt strong. "You been working out."

Nick stood back and started flexing. "A little somethin' but you know I've always been buff."

I laughed because I once saw some pictures of Nick as a young teen. He used to be kind of puny. "Yeah, Bootney Farnsworth."

As I took off my coat I noticed Nick sitting with his legs unusually far apart.

"What are you doing?" He had a big grin on his face as he began thrusting his pelvis into the air.

"You're joking, right? I just got in the house."

"Come on, Asha, I haven't had sex since I last saw you and I'm in the mood."

I laughed at him as he winded his hips seductively and patted the space next to him. "You a damn liar. What happened to Baby Girl?"

His face contorted in disgust. "Baby Girl?"

"Yes, Nick, the one you said you were going to marry."

"Asha, you like two sevens stuck together."

I crossed my arms and waited for the payoff. "What does that mean, Nick?"

"It means that you are a square! I ain't say nuthin' to you about marryin Baby Girl."

"But you told me she was so fine you were gonna make her your wife."

His eyes roamed over my face and his tone became serious. "I wanted to gauge your reaction, sweetheart."

I sensed that Nick was waiting for me to say some specific thing, but since I didn't know what it was, I kept my mouth shut.

He switched back to gangsta-thug talk. "Besides, I probably said wifey not wife."

"What is a wifey?"

"A wifey is just a girlfriend you like a lot and you don't want her to go out there fuckin' around, so you give her a title and she sticks around forever and ever."

"What about getting engaged until you figure things out?"

Nick's already big eyes popped out of his head further. "Oh, no, no, no! You crazy! A wifey don't get no ring, girl!"

"Is that true, Nick? Is that what this kid says?"

"Yup."

"Wait; so let me get this straight. So basically a "wifey" is an insurance policy for a brother who has no intention of actually making any real commitment to his girlfriend but has decided he doesn't want her messing around with other people while he does whatever he wants? What kind of sorry-ass woman would agree to an arrangement like that?"

Nick thought about it a few seconds. "The kind that's in love."

I laughed hysterically at the creativity of my brethren. "How old is Baby Girl?"

"She about our age."

"And you told her she was your wifey?"

"Yup."

I was starting to wonder what was real and what was Nick fooling around. "There is no way any female over the age of sixteen would listen to some wifey bullshit. Are you fooling around with young girls?"

"Aw, come on, now, you trippin'. I don't mess wit no little girls. I ain't R. Kelly."

"Where is this woman really from, Nick?" I could barely breathe from laughing so hard.

"She's really from Houston but it's a real poor part of town."

"Figures that some ghetto broad would go for that bullshit. Or maybe that Texas sun has cooked her brain. Why are you scrapin' from the bottom of the barrel, Nick? Are you afraid to settle down with a nice, smart woman?"

"No, but you won't marry me and those chickenheads don't take a lot of work!"

"Stop it, Nick."

He grinned a foolish thug grin. "You right, girl. All this serious talk is makin' my head hurt. Come over here and let me lay it down!"

"Not on my nice leather sofa we're not."

I got up and lay in his lap. I felt his erection growing.

"I want you right here on your Seaman's couch," he said.

I play-smacked him. "Nothing from Seaman's furniture store would ever be allowed in here."

"Well, let's do sumthin' before I bust a hole in your skull wit my pee pee."

He had to wait until I showered and freshened up.

It took me twenty minutes to cut my pubic hair into a cute little heart shape. By the time I had shaved, washed, and oiled, Nick had practically given up hope.

He took one look at me and the gangsta flew out the window. He was Nick Seabrook—jazz afficionado and lover extraordinaire—once more.

"Wow, you look sooo sexy," he said, grabbing me around my waist.

I could tell he appreciated the silky feel of my copper chemise as his hands slid over my curves. "Asha, you smell wonderful."

We locked lips and then he took my hand and led me to the bedroom.

It was something about the way he led me into the bedroom

that made me feel like one hundred percent woman, like some sensuous mythical creature.

Nick slipped the thin straps of my gown off my shoulders and asked me to simply stand in front of him so he could appreciate what he saw. It was awkward at first, especially since he was still in his boxers, but when I saw the twinkle of genuine admiration in his eyes I no longer minded. He started to slide out of his boxers in front of me, seductively, in a way that only Nick could do it without the act coming across soft or gay.

"Let me pull down your boxers," I said.

He smiled and nodded as I slid them down to the floor. His penis jumped excitedly. "Lie down," he said.

I climbed on the bed and lay on my back. I was shocked when Nick began sucking and licking my toes as he massaged my calves. He took time with every inch of my body, rubbing, petting, and stroking me into oblivion. I was surprised that he performed oral sex but he did and it was fantastic. He hadn't even entered me yet and I had two orgasms; but nothing prepared me for the actual intercourse. Nick seemed to hit all the right areas as he prodded my inner walls. It felt so good I just didn't want to stop grinding down on him.

"Oh, my God!" I yelled as he kept thrusting into me.

"You just had a G-spot orgasm, that's all," he said matter-of-factly.

I flopped back on the bed satiated like I had never been before.

I wasn't surprised that Nick fell asleep since he had driven all the way from Houston.

I took a shower, moistened my eyes with Visine and lay down on the sofa to catch up on my reading. It's been a long time since I had a quiet Friday night. Just when my book started getting interesting the doorman called to say my sister was on her way up.

Girlfriend looked a mess! Before I could fully digest the swollen eyes, disheveled clothes, and tearstained face, she stomped past me. "I never want to see or speak to Phil again as long as I live!"

I couldn't have been more shocked if Saundra had said she was going to become a hooker, working the streets near the river on Eleventh Avenue. "This is the first time you've ever complained about Phil," I said, pushing her into my living room. "What on earth did you two fight about?"

"Please don't ask," she answered miserably, falling onto my red leather couch like it didn't cost me over two grand. "I had to leave and there is nowhere else for me to go."

To my horror, she covered her face with both hands and burst into sobs that were so heartrending I would have given up all my jewelry to make her stop. Instead, I sat down beside her, pulled her head onto my chest, and cried with her. What had Phil done to my sister? My head started throbbing as I searched my mental Rolodex for the name of a gangster-type dude who had spent some time with me two years ago. What the hell was his name? His face was still clear in my memory: Light-skin, high cheekbones, and eyes that never conveyed an emotion. He gave me five thousand dollars in cash and an emerald necklace when he split. A dangerous motherfucka. Just what I needed to take Phil down if he had made the mistake of beating up Saundra.

She was rocking back and forth. The way she was holding her stomach filled me with rage. "What the fuck did Phil do to you, Saundra? I'll kill the sonofabitch."

Saundra looked into my eyes for a moment. "He didn't hurt me physically if that is what you're thinking. I swear it. He didn't lay a hand on me and that worthless bastard is definitely not worth you going to jail for. I just need to lie down."

"Okay, let's get some sleep, sweetie, and we can talk in the morning," I told her quietly. "Nick is in my bed but I'm going in there and put his ass out."

"Which one is Nick?" She sniffled.

"The one with the huge trust fund." I put an arm around her shoulder.

She pulled away from me and hunched over, holding her stomach again. "It doesn't matter. Let him stay. I'll be fine out here."

"Where is Yero? Did he drive you here? Do you want me to call him?"

"Fuck him," she spat. "I'm not marrying anybody. He probably has secrets I don't know about, too. I hate all men. Every last one of them."

My heart almost stopped beating. Saundra calling Phil a worthless bastard? Fuck Yero? What in Sam's hell was going on?

"Saundra . . ."

"Stop talking. Leave me alone."

Saundra lay down with her back to me. Her shoulders shook, so I knew that she was still weeping.

Chapter 31

PHIL

Saundra was gone.

As soon as I saw her standing in the doorway, my brain froze. As if in slow motion, I saw Saundra's shock turn to disbelief, then revulsion. I felt my own hands sliding blue jeans over my feet and up my legs. I felt the soft, nubby carpet under my feet as I ran downstairs and then the pain of the graveled driveway. My elbow kept moving back and forth like somebody had it on a string and it took me a minute to realize that Pastor Hoffman was pulling on it. Saundra's cab disappeared into the night and then the fuzziness disappeared. The whole thing became enormously plain.

I had lost her forever.

My Saundra . . .

Pastor Hoffman watched as a now fully dressed Hugo removed my elbow from his grasp and led me firmly back inside my own home.

"I'm so sorry," he kept saying as I collapsed on the living room sofa. "It'll be all right. You'll see . . ."

But it wasn't going to be all right, and when Hugo said it for a third time, I told him to shut the fuck up. My skull began to split from the inside and I clutched one of the pillows as though it was the key to maintaining my sanity. My eyes closed and then something cold and wet was pressed against my lips. It was Hugo . . .

trying to get me to drink something. I slapped it out of his hands. "Get the hell outta my goddamn house. I ain't had nothin' but problems since I met your motherfuckin' Puerto Rican ass!"

That was a lie.

The problem started in the first grade. At age six I had a crush on Willie, a little redheaded boy who could jump hopscotch as well as any boy on our block. When I kissed Willie on the mouth, Dad was furious but Mom told him that he was just being ridiculous. We were just kids doing silly kid things.

Things were pretty cool until seventh grade when a boy named Ernest moved to Dayton from a small town in Virginia. It took me a couple of weeks to work up the courage but I finally confessed my feelings for him. He beat the living shit out of me and told his parents. I lied my ass off when Dad confronted me. It was my word against Ernest's and, since Dad couldn't prove anything, he let it go. But he watched every move I made after that. Mom did, too.

In high school, my speed and build made me the football team's star quarterback. The fact that I never asked my dates for any poontang earned me a reputation as "Dayton's perfect gentleman." Dad was real suspicious of that reputation. His solution? He took me to a whorehouse and left me in a raggedy-ass room with an ugly-assed old woman that I wouldn't have touched for any amount of money in the world. In fact, I reached into my pocket and gave her every cent I had. All she had to do was assure my father that I was straight and one hell of a stud.

That stunt bought me two years of peace and a genuinely warm friendship developed between me and Dad. I adored him and reveled in the pride he felt about my grades and the legendary moves that I made on the football field.

On the night of my high school graduation, all hell broke loose.

Young, drunk, and careless. That is the only way to explain why I got caught in the backseat of a car with my tongue halfway down the throat of a guy I had been seeing on the quiet for about six months.

Dad caught me and told me to get out of Dayton and keep

going. He didn't care where or how. But if I ever set foot on his property again to say good-bye to Mama, get my clothes . . . anything . . . he would blow my brains out and turn himself in to the cops.

So I left home wearing a suit underneath my liquor stained cap and gown with only twenty dollars in my pocket. My lover bought me a bus ticket to New York.

Dayton, Ohio, had not prepared me for hustling through a series of odd jobs in Times Square or the flophouse that was the only place a minimum wage slave like me could afford to stay in. The only good thing about that period of my life was the freedom to date any guy who appealed to me without worrying about Dad's eagle eye.

I called Mama a couple of times but she hung up every time she heard my voice.

"Phil, don't cry." Hugo was kneeling on the floor with his head on my stomach. Cry? I touched my face. It was wet. My chest was heaving. "Hugo, go on home. I need to be by myself." The voice didn't sound like mine. It sounded heavy, raspy.

"No," he said. "You might do something crazy."

So we cried together until the sun came up.

Chapter 32

EVELYN

Since I was doing the four P.M. to midnight shift as a favor for someone else, I was still in bed when Mama, who was dressed for work, peeked into my bedroom. "Honey, Phil is downstairs. Is he sick or something? He don't look too good."

Phil? He was supposed to be on eight A.M. to four P.M. today. I looked at the clock. It was eight-thirty. "Maybe he has a cold or something. Don't worry about it."

She kissed me on the cheek and left.

I yawned and took a moment to brush my teeth and run a wet cloth over my face before going down to the kitchen. I expected to find him boiling water for tea or something. Instead, he was pacing back and forth, mumbling to himself. He looked at me and then down at the floor.

"Good morning, sweetie," I said with a smile. I reached forward to hug him and he stepped back like I had leprosy.

"Sit down, Evelyn. We need to talk."

It had been thirty-two years since I'd felt this type of burning in my stomach. Back then, the fire that licked at my guts was caused by the tear-filled eyes of a camp counselor as she took my hands and told me that my father was dead but I had to be brave for my mother's sake. From the expression on Phil's face, I knew that the bad news had something to do with Saundra. I gripped the edge of the table for strength.

"What is it?" I whispered.

"Well, I have good news and bad news. Which do you want first?" He tried to smile but couldn't.

Making any type of decision was simply impossible. Not with Phil's puffy bloodshot eyes shifting from side to side. Not when his shoulders were slumped forward so far that he was almost toppling over. Not with his hands shaking like those of a thirty year alcoholic in need of a drink.

I felt woozy.

Phil sighed and looked away. "It's like this . . . um . . . Josephine is never going to come through with her share of the money so . . . um . . . so I'm going to give it to you. It doesn't mean we're business partners and it's not a loan. It's a gift. Okay?"

On any other day, I would have been clicking my heels in the air but the air was loaded with something else. Something tragic. It made me mute.

Phil cleared his throat. "That's the good news. But . . . um . . . look here, Evelyn . . . the bad news . . . well . . . It's about you and me . . . Well, I'm sorry but . . . um . . . we have to break up."

I was thunderstruck. "What?"

"Evelyn, what I've done to you is wrong."

What had he done? What was he talking about?

I tried to stand up but my legs wouldn't support me and so I dropped back down in the chair. "Phil, what is going on?"

"Evelyn, I feel awful about all this."

A vein in my temple began to throb. "Awful about what?"

"About not telling you a long time ago that I don't want to get married."

He wasn't giving me any options. "This doesn't make sense, Phil. How do you know that I want to break up over this?"

There was no answer and that only meant one thing. "There's someone else. Right?"

He sighed heavily. "Yes, there is. I'm really sorry, Evelyn."

There was no feeling anywhere in my body. "How long have you been seeing her?"

"A long, long time."

My fingers sprung loose from the edge of the table and flew to my pockets. Where the hell was my gun? It wasn't there. Because I was still in my bathrobe. I jumped up from the table and headed upstairs to my bedroom to get it and put every single bullet right through his lying, cheating heart.

Phil grabbed me on the landing. "Evelyn, calm down. It's not like you think. Please let me explain."

I struggled against his strong grip. "Let me go!"

"Evelyn, it's not another woman."

"But you just said . . ."

"I said it was someone else. I didn't say it was a woman."

My frenzied thrashing gave way to absolute and utter shock. "WHAT?"

He released me and used his body to block my climb upstairs. "Evelyn, you know how it is in the department. I had to lie. I still have to. You know that. Believe me, if I did anything else for a living, things would have been different. All this sneaking and hiding and deceiving everybody would never have happened."

Phil was blocking the path to the gun but we had a drawer full of knives in the kitchen. I took off and when I turned to face him again, it was with a butcher knife in my hand. He just stood there looking sad but I knew he wasn't going to let me hurt him. We were at an impasse.

"Gay? How long have you been gay?"

"All my life," he said simply.

"So I was just a beard?"

He took a step toward me. "Evelyn, you're smart, funny, beautiful, kind. You're the most wonderful woman on earth."

If this son of a bitch ended with "and any man would be lucky to have you" I would lunge at him with the knife and somehow, even though he was stronger, manage to plunge it right through his heart.

"Shut the fuck up, Phil! How could you do this to me for six whole years? And how did you manage to sneak away to meet men when you were always at work or with Saundra or over here?"

He looked startled. "Sneak away to meet men?"

"Yes. Or did you order them by mail?"

"Oh, no! I haven't been cruising men . . . I . . . it's just one person . . ."

I didn't want to hear the details. "I don't believe you could do something so brutal and nasty to me. Why me? Why did you pick me to be your beard?"

He opened his mouth to answer and then shut it.

"How could you be so cruel to another human being, Phil?"

"I'm sorry, Evelyn. I don't know what else to say."

I threw the knife and it hit him in the face before clattering to the floor.

"Get out, Phil. Get out and don't ever speak to me again."

"Evelyn . . ." He stopped a moment, took a deep breath, and the rest of the words rushed out. "Would you do one last thing for me?"

No, this motherfucker did not just ask me to do him a favor. I stopped breathing and just stared at him.

"Would you please help Saundra through this? Not for me. I don't deserve anything. Please do it for her?"

Saundra!

"You mean she didn't know?"

He blinked. "She does now. Saundra walked in on us last night and ran away. I'm sure she is at Asha's house."

"Walked in? You mean that . . ."

"Yes," he said simply. "Hugo and I were having sex. It was the first time in my house. I swear it. She was supposed to spend the night with Yero. I don't know why . . ."

Hugo!

"STOP!" I screamed. "JUST STOP!

"You're right. It's too much to ask." He turned to leave.

That's when I snatched up the microwave, ran up behind him and used it to club him right in the back of the head.

Chapter 33

SAUNDRA

I sobbed on that cold leather, my chest rising and falling until it hurt, tears racing down my face and drenching my blouse. I wept for Evelyn, who loved a man who would never love her or any other woman. I wept for Mama, who had lain with a man who was obviously just experimenting to see if he could stand making love to a female.

Finally, when I could cry no more, I closed my eyes tight and wished that I could fall asleep and wake up to find out it was all a nightmare. If not that, then that I could wake up in some alternate universe where Asha and I were still little girls with Mama making banana pancakes in the kitchen. Oh, to find myself back on the bottom bunk in the small bedroom of our old apartment with Asha on the top bunk reading under the covers with a flashlight, listening to bags of garbage drop from the window of some lazy tenant down into the alley. To be small, adored, and ignorant of just how ugly and deceitful the world could be.

I heard Asha's bedroom door opening and knew she was coming to check on me, so I regulated my breathing and pretended to be asleep.

She stood there for a moment, kissed me on the cheek and went back to her room.

It occurred to me that she would probably take the next day off from work and I didn't want her to. I didn't want to talk. I didn't want to plan. There was no way I was ever going to tell my sister the truth about Phil. I was too ashamed.

So, I waited another hour and then tiptoed around until I found a pen and some paper. I wrote a note to her in big letters. It said:

> Asha,
>   I know you mean well but go to work in the morning. I need time to be alone and sort some stuff out. Please don't be stubborn about this, Asha. Respect my wishes and I promise to call before you go to lunch so you know that I'm all right.
>
>   Love,
>   Saundra

I taped that note to the bathroom door.

I woke up the next morning with a soft pillow under my face and a comforter spread over my body and up to my neck. There was a note from Asha on the coffee table along with her house keys and a credit card.

> Hey, Sis—
>   Hope you're feeling better this morning. Take the Visa and go shopping. That always lifts my spirits. Call me at work like you promised.
>
>   Hugs and kisses,
>   Asha

What a horrible night! There were no more tears left. Just a dull headache, sore limbs and a thousand questions.

How long had Phil been gay?

Should I tell poor Evelyn?

Would Asha let my pets live here too?

What skeletons did Yero have in his closet that he would have sprung on me after twenty years of marriage and five kids?

The answers to those questions would have to wait. It was time to call Yero. He was behind the stamp counter now so I dialed his cell. The phone rang three times before he answered.

"Yero?"

"Saundra! Baby, I'm really sorry about yesterday. What I said about Asha was just plain wrong. Do you forgive me?"

"Yero, we need to talk."

"Okay. I'll come over after work."

"Don't."

"What?"

"Don't go to Phil's house."

"Phil? When did you start calling your father by his first name?"

"I've moved out of Phil's house."

His voice rose in fear. "Baby, where are you?"

"Living with Asha."

He was silent for a second. "What happened?"

"Nothing I ever want to talk about."

"Saundra . . ."

I cut him off. "Yero, I need a whole lot of space right now. No relationship. No wedding. Nothing but space."

"Whoa! I'm leaving work and coming to see you. Now."

My voice was steel. "Don't. I mean it, Yero. I won't be here."

"Saundra, why are you treating me like this?"

He sounded so pitiful.

"Yero, I'm sorry, but I don't really know who you are."

"Who I am? Saundra, are you having a nervous breakdown? Put Asha on the phone."

"Asha is at work."

"I'm on my way."

Yero hung up before I could say another word.

I heard footsteps behind me and then a deep male voice said, "Another brother bites the dust!"

Too frightened to even scream, I whirled around and came face-to-face with a six-foot stranger who was emerging from Asha's bedroom.

"Oh, my God! Who are you?"

He looked confused and then backed up, holding his hands above his head. "Nick Seabrook. Asha's friend."

My throat felt dry. "How did you get in?"

"I was already here when you came last night."

I vaguely remembered Asha mentioning a man in her bed. "Oh. Right."

He lowered his arms. "Don't start tripping and shoot me, okay?"

"Okay."

He sighed. "Jeez! You put a pillow under a sister's head so her cheek don't get scratched on leather and cover her up with a blanket so she doesn't freeze to death and then in the morning she wants to kill you."

I went back to the sofa. "Sorry."

He sat down beside me. "So, who was the brother that you just kicked to the curb?"

"My ex-fiancé."

Ex-fiancé. The phrase hung in the air until it made me double over in pain.

Nick dropped his jocular air. "There isn't a man on earth who is worth that kind of agony," he said quietly. "Try to forget whatever he has done to you."

"He didn't do anything," I wailed.

"Excuse me?"

"Well, he did do something. I just don't know what it is yet and I have no intention of sticking around to find out."

Nick stared at me and said nothing but I didn't feel like explaining.

Chapter 34

ASHA

I was calculating a spreadsheet when Kevin rang to say my sister
was on the phone.

"Saundra, are you all right?"

"Yes. I just called to warn you that my ex might show up at
Macy's today."

"Yero? Coming here? Why?"

"Probably to talk you into getting us back together but I'm
telling you right now that I don't want to hear it."

"Fine. No skin off my back."

"Asha, you've been right all along."

"About Yero?"

"About all men. Fuck them all."

She slammed the phone down in my ear.

It was such a relief to hear Saundra sounding like herself again.
The old Saundra from high school, the one who used to scratch
up faces and hit people over the head with bottles and shit.

All this earth mother stuff is just a mask for the tough girl she's
always been. I'm not saying that it's acceptable for a grown
woman to act out like she used to when she got frustrated, but in
a way, it was refreshing to hear the old Saundra's voice and not
that of Lao Tzu or Iyanla Vanzant. Evelyn was the one who told
her to learn to "channel her strength" with meditation, chanting,

affirmations and all that other bullshit. That's fine if that is who a person is, but Saundra was never like that. She was always the one out of the two of us that faced things head on without the gloss. I always admired her bluntness but when she started trying to be someone she wasn't, things got weird. The funny thing is, she never stopped being up front with me—just with herself.

If Saundra is beginning to wake up out of her yoga zone, then I feel sorry for Yero because he hasn't seen rage yet.

I knew Yero was going to end up full of shit because all those so called "righteous brothers" are. All they do is talk shit about up-lifting the race, grow their dreads, sport militant T-shirts and don't end up doing shit.

Dante used to wear those leather medallions back in high school, the ones with the continent of Africa painted red, black, and green with a gold lion in the center. Sometimes he wore several of them at the same time and had the nerve to blast Gang Starr, Poor Righteous Teachers and Brand Nubian all the time, and look what he did to his so-called "African Queen."

If he had done that to the old Saundra, she would have castrated him like I should have.

Chapter 35

SAUNDRA

After throwing Nick out and calling my sister, I decided to shower and then find an organic food store. There was nothing in Asha's refrigerator that I would even consider putting in my mouth.

The phone rang several times and the Caller ID let me know that it was Phil, then Evelyn calling from her car, then Phil, then Evelyn two more times.

Phil could go to hell with his nasty ass but I would return Evelyn's call when I get back.

The cold air felt good and helped clear my head as I wove in and out of all the side streets on my way to the open market a few blocks away. I grabbed a shopping cart and started throwing healthy food into it: prickly pear extract, six-grain bread, tofu, vegan pizza dough, eight Roma tomatoes, coarse salt, veggie burgers, soy milk, vegan maple syrup, Rapadura whole organic sugar, Gimmie Lean sausage, Vegemite gravy, soy milk, vegan banana pancakes, un-chicken broth, Almost cheese, Just like chicken, brown rice and non-dairy ice cream.

On the walk back, I realized that although the truth about Phil's sexuality had stunned me beyond belief, it wasn't what hurt the most. Being gay goes against the laws of nature but it isn't evil.

What really hurt was the way he and Hugo had deceived both me and Evelyn for all these years.

Chapter 36

EVELYN

I feel exhausted. Sick of Mama asking me what the matter is and sick of pretending to be sick so I don't have to go to work. Sick of thinking about Phil, Saundra, and Hugo. Sick of wondering how I'm going to make the retreat happen because I would never take money from Phil for anything now. You can't build a wellness center with funds from the devil.

So I've come to see Saundra. She will know that it is a good-bye without me having to say so. She will notice that my skin, normally the color of butterscotch, is now a blotchy, sickly stale butter. She will see the slight bend to my shoulders, which wasn't there before, and she will know that I have to get far far away from here.

I told Saundra that I would come over around noon.

When she opened the door, there was a new set to her jaw, determination in her eyes and the youngish enthusiasm was gone. In a way, it was comforting to know that Saundra had grown up—albeit the hard way—and would be able to take care of herself from now on.

I said hello, managed a smile and we hugged.

She started talking as soon as our butts hit Asha's leather sofa.

"I'm so sorry, Evelyn. What Phil has done to you is unconscionable."

"Don't apologize for your father's treachery, Saundra. It isn't healthy."

She nodded and fell back with her arms folded across her chest. "I'll never forgive him."

"Then you didn't learn anything from me, Saundra. You have to forgive him for your own peace of mind."

My words sounded hollow probably because I knew it would take an in-person visit from the Dalai Lama himself to make me ever forgive Phil.

She tried to put her arms around me but something deep inside me just couldn't accept the gesture. Her hands fell away and she looked uncertain.

"Evelyn, what can I do to help you?"

I tried to laugh at that but it came out as a bark. Was I losing my mind? "Nothing, baby. Just try to understand if I don't make it to your wedding. I'll certainly be there in spirit."

"I'm not getting married. Yero and I broke up."

Now I had to pull her into my arms. "Don't be a fool, Saundra," I whispered. "Yero is the real thing and you deserve no less than a good man like him. Promise me that you'll reconsider?"

She cried quietly. "I promise."

We made a little small talk but I felt uncomfortable. It was time for me to go. My job was done.

Chapter 37

ASHA

Yero showed up just as I was heading out for lunch. I expected him to look sad or angry but not dazed and confused.

He looked over at me from the armchair near my desk while I sat with my arms folded, trying to look stern and official.

"Thank you for seeing me, Asha," he said in a very tired voice.

"What happened to Saundra last night?" I demanded.

"I didn't see Saundra last night. We had a little spat earlier in the evening and I went home. She called this morning to say she had moved out of Phil's house and the wedding was off."

"It must have been more than a little spat for her to kick you to the curb."

His eyes filled with pain. "Then she really means it? We're through?"

I shrugged. "Looks that way."

"But why?"

I couldn't understand why he looked so bewildered. "Evidently, it felt like more than a spat to my sister."

"No way," he shouted.

"Lower your voice," I whispered. "Are you trying to get me fired?"

"There is no way that Saundra would call off our wedding because of that petty mess."

"What did the two of you argue about?"

He looked embarrassed. "I can't tell you."

"Yech! That means it's a sexual issue and, you're right. I don't want to know."

"Asha, look at me."

I looked into his eyes and saw fear.

"I swear to you that I don't know why Saundra is so pissed off at me. I swear that the words we exchanged yesterday were not the type that would make any woman call off her own wedding."

It was clear he was telling the truth.

"What the hell is going on?"

"That's what I've been trying to tell you. I don't have any idea."

"What was the fight between Saundra and Phil about?" I asked sharply.

Yero stood up so quickly that he banged his knee hard on my desk and let out a yelp of pain.

"Saundra had a fight with Phil?"

"You didn't know?"

He shook his head in denial and slumped back into the chair with one hand covering his face. "Saundra is going to tell me to my face that she doesn't want me anymore. That's the only way to get rid of me."

My head started to hurt. There was only one thing left to do. I pressed the speaker button so that Yero could hear the conversation and dialed Phil's number. He answered on the first ring.

"Saundra?"

"No. It's Asha. I'm sitting here with Yero and we need to talk to you."

"Is Saundra okay?"

I took a deep breath. "No; she is most definitely not okay. What the hell went on out there last night?"

He groaned. "Put Saundra on the phone."

"She isn't here Phil and I'm not telling you anything else about her condition until you answer the question."

Phil started to cry. "Please tell me that she didn't try to . . . to . . . kill herself or something?"

"Kill herself?"

Yero and I exchanged frightened glances. In less than a second we were both crying.

"Phil, what happened?"

"You son of a bitch!" screamed Yero. "What the fuck is wrong with Saundra?"

"Phil, you have to tell me what happened."

"Saundra," he gasped.

I realized we were getting nowhere. "Phil, my sister did not try to kill herself and, physically she seems fine . . ."

"Thank God."

"But something has shaken her up mentally. Yero and I can't help her if we don't know what's wrong."

"She probably doesn't want you to know."

I wanted to tear his head off. "Know what?"

"Saundra stumbled on a secret last night. Something that I didn't plan to tell her until after graduation and the wedding. I'm sorry."

A secret.

I wiped my eyes. "What does the secret have to do with Yero?"

There was a pause. "Yero? It has nothing to do with him."

This was some crazy shit. "Yes, it does. Saundra told him that she doesn't want to see him and the wedding is off."

"Sweet Jesus," he moaned. "Tell my daughter that I love her. Tell her I never meant to hurt her like this. Tell her not to start hating all men because of me."

By now I was shaking the telephone console in frustration as Yero massaged my shoulders. "Phil, if you love Saundra, you've got to tell me the secret so I can help her."

"Asha, if I do that she'll hate me forever."

"Then what are we supposed to do, Phil?"

He whispered something to someone and then came back to the phone. "Saundra needs your love and some professional help. Yero should just be patient."

"Professional help? You mean a shrink?"

He sighed. "Yes, a psychiatrist. I'll pay for it."

"Put Evelyn on the phone."

"Evelyn is not here. She and I broke up, too."

I didn't know what else to say.

Chapter 38

SAUNDRA

I managed to squeak through my final exams and complete registration for the upcoming and last semester. God must have just held my hand each step of the way because it all felt like an out-of-body experience. Asha has been real sweet about everything and she must have said something to Phil because he has backed off.

Yero is another story. Up until yesterday, he was showing up every day, but I kept telling the doorman not to let him upstairs.

Christmas is one week away. I'm amazed at how much has happened to all of us in just a few weeks. Hopefully, Nick will take Asha away on a winter vacation. I'd rather sleep through the holidays than pretend to be cheery for her sake.

Asha gave me some pamphlets about where to go for grief counseling, the warning signs of clinical depression and a book called *Letting Go and Moving On*. On top of all that, one night she pushed a business card into my hand. It was a referral to some psychiatrist on the upper West Side. I hope she doesn't hit me with any more of that stuff. What I really need is to get out of this city and that will happen in May—right after the graduation ceremony. A train ticket to Los Angeles will be pinned to the blouse underneath my gown.

A few days ago, Asha wanted to know if there was anything I

needed. Yes—all my clothes, pets, books, design equipment and the sewing machine. And you know what? Her friend Nick rented a small truck, they changed into matching overalls with matching blue caps and zoomed off into the night. They brought back everything except Blinky. Asha is terrified of snakes.

In fact, Asha doesn't like the turtles, snails, fish, or my hamster. So, she avoids the living room and spends most of her time in the bathroom, bedroom, or kitchen.

It isn't fair to restrict someone else's space so I'm going to surprise her by selling all the animals. I just need to get through the holidays first.

Chapter 39

ASHA

I called ahead and by the time Nick and I showed up for Saundra's things, Phil was nowhere in sight. There was just a very sad-looking Hugo. He watched silently as we carried stuff out.

Yero and I had a pact. We would share clues and solve the mystery together.

Saundra still refused to tell me what happened; she wasn't taking Yero's calls or letting him come upstairs. All she did was brood, take long walks, read and meditate. I plan to give her this one last night of grief and then I'm putting a stop to it.

To my surprise, Saundra was on the phone one night when I got home from work. I waved at her and she responded by blowing me a kiss.

She kept running her mouth as I threw my coat on a chair and hunted around among all the strange items in my refrigerator in the hopes of finding one normal beer.

"You finished the collection! Twenty-five poems that you're satisfied with?" she asked into the receiver. "I'm so incredibly happy for you! Oh, you're giving me way too much credit. Encouragement is one thing but you did all the work. Yes, I'd love to read them. Well, I'm living here with my sister now. As a matter of fact, she just walked in." She waved me toward the phone. "Well, it was nice talking to you."

"Who is it?" I whispered.

"Derrick. He said you left a message on his machine."

"Whatever," I said, angry that it had taken him weeks to return my call.

"Asha, how are you?" His voice sounded lazy, like he had just smoked a joint.

"Wonderful," I made my voice sound light and devil-may-care.

"Sorry it took me so long to get back at you but I've been focused on a project. Just wrapped it up last night." \

He was cute, sexy and had a tight ass but my life had changed a lot since that night at Tea Party. Getting him into my bed didn't matter as much as getting Saundra out of it. "Don't sweat it, Derrick. My sister had told me all about your poetry collection."

Saundra's jaw dropped at the lie.

"So, what did you want?" he asked.

WHAT? This man had seen me live and in person! He should have been hoping to take me out on a date. Praying that I would let him climb into bed with me. Instead, his voice was rife with disinterest and he was merely returning a call to his friend's sister out of politeness. Oh, no! The brother was gay and I'd made a complete fool of myself.

I had to save face. I thought of a quick lie and my tone changed to regretful. "Oh, this is really too bad. I was having some folks over for drinks because one of my girlfriends was here from out of town. To make a long story short, you seemed like her type and I wanted to hook y'all up. She's gone now. I'm sorry."

"Very interesting." He sounded amused.

Time to get brotherman off the phone. "Thanks for calling back, Derrick."

"No problem, have a good night."

Saundra was puttering around the kitchen, not looking me directly in the eye. "So how was your day?"

"Work is work," I snapped.

"Are you mad at me about something? Let me make you a cup of cinnamon tea."

"Cut the crap, Saundra. Your little joke wasn't funny. Why didn't you tell me that Derrick was gay?"

"Because he isn't. The truth is that he is into white girls so don't take his rejection personally."

"Why didn't you tell me?"

Saundra's eyes narrowed in anger. "Because I was tired of your irresponsible antics with men, that's why."

The self-righteous bitch.

Chapter 40

SAUNDRA

Having my possessions and talking to Derrick had made me feel a lot better. At least I felt like I was back among the living.

The next evening Asha insisted that I go out to dinner with her. Even though, I wasn't feeling well enough to sit around some fancy restaurant, she wouldn't take no for an answer.

"Saundra, will you fix me something to drink while I change?"

I twisted some lemon into a glass of chilled Evian water.

She looked at the glass and then back at me. "Thanks for the lemon. I'm feeling a little risqué tonight."

Oh, so she had wanted a glass of rum. I thought she was just thirsty.

It went without saying that she was going to order alcohol in the restaurant. Why did she have to drink so much?

I forgot her warning and flopped down on her Ethan Allen you-shouldn't-flop-down-on-it leather couch. I picked up a crystal carving of the Eiffel Tower. "Asha, I've been meaning to ask, where did you get this? It's gorgeous."

"Oh, Brent gave me that. He's an executive at Tiffany's. They have a lot of those kinds of crystal carvings. By the way, he plans to take me with him to Paris after the holidays."

"He works for Tiffany's!" I didn't even know they let black folks up in the ranks there."

"They take good care of him. He has no limit on his corporate expense account."

"He sounds perfect for you, why don't you marry him?"

"For the same reason you refuse to have a nice juicy steak. The very idea just makes me sick."

I sucked my teeth. "So when are you going to Gay Paree?"

"As soon as he gets back from Aspen with his wife."

Aw, man! "His wife?"

"Wait till you see these emerald earrings he bought me."

"You're awful."

"Yeah, I know. I'll be right back." she grinned.

She couldn't wait to show them off. They were the most exquisite emeralds I had ever seen—oval shaped, nicely cut with diamond studded frames.

She dropped them into my outstretched hand. "Look. Aren't they beautiful?"

I peered into my hand and then gave the pair back to her along with the truth. "No, Asha, they're not. You slept with a married man to get them."

"No I didn't, he gave them to me as a present. Besides, I'm not the one who promised to love and cherish that woman, *he* did. If he doesn't respect his vows, why should I?"

My stomach clenched in disapproval but I was staying in her house so I decided to change the subject. "Where are we having dinner tonight?" I asked.

"Jade Crown."

I smiled because Jade Crown wasn't too fancy schmancy. They served the best Chinese food in the city for a very reasonable price.

After our surprisingly traffic-less cab ride to Sixty-Third Street and Columbus Avenue we arrived in front of Jade Crown in exactly fifteen minutes. To our relief, as soon as the heavy glass doors of the restaurant closed behind us the noise from the street vanished, leaving us with just the peaceful tinkling of traditional Chinese music. We were greeted cordially by a tiny woman with an extraordinarily flat butt and escorted to a small red booth by the window.

The restaurant was dimly lit, warm, and crowded. There were oil paintings of magnificent pagodas and giddy laughter from a couple sitting out of eye shot. It was hard not to think about Yero. I pushed him way back into a dim corner of my mind.

As I sipped my tea, I noticed twinkles of mirth in Asha's light brown eyes. "What's on your mind?"

"I'm thinking about my trip to Paris."

"Why?"

"I'm thinking about what a diva I'll be when I get there." She grinned.

I laughed because I knew she was right.

"So what do you plan to see first?"

"The Eiffel Tower, of course, but I'm really excited about seeing the Montmartre and Montparrase districts."

"That's where all those jazz singers did their thing, right?"

"Yeah, those neighborhoods *were* the Jazz Age in Paris."

"You'll probably find nothing there." I said.

"Why do you say that?"

"You'll probably look just like those white folks that tour Harlem on buses every weekend, looking for a way of life that has vanished."

We both had a hearty laugh. "I don't think so, Saundra."

"What I can't believe is their lack of shame as they ride through like they're on safari. We went shopping up there a few months ago and I couldn't believe it. Harlem has once again become some kind of romanticized hub for a new generation of primativists." I stopped in mid-rant. "Asha, some guy keeps staring over here every time his date isn't looking."

She swiveled her head around and then giggled. "It's Brent. Come with me to the ladies' room so I can get a look at his wife."

I didn't want any part of this. "What makes you think that the woman is his wife?"

Asha insisted.

We walked slowly toward their table and Asha stopped, looking surprised. He was with a Polynesian-looking woman who looked like she could be a model.

"Hi, Brent! How are you?" Asha said cheerfully.

Brent's eyes got extraterrestrial in size. "Hey, Asha!"

She actually extended her hand to the woman. "Hi, I'm Asha. This is my sister Saundra."

She shook our hands and smiled uneasily. "I'm Lula."

To say I was uncomfortable would be a huge understatement.

"Nice to meet you Lula. Well, I'll see you later, Brent. You enjoy the rest of your meal."

We turned around and walked at a normal pace towards the ladies' room. When we got into the bathroom we checked all the stalls to make sure no one heard us.

"I can't believe it," Asha said, pacing back and forth. "That woman is not his wife."

"Surely you didn't think you were the only one."

"What are you talking about?"

"The fact that you're upset about whoever that woman is."

She waved a hand impatiently. "I couldn't care less who Brent sleeps with. Didn't you notice her ears? He gave that girl the same earrings except hers are ruby. Why did I get the emeralds and she got the rubies?"

"Perhaps because that really is his wife," I replied sarcastically.

We collapsed against each other laughing at her greed.

"No, Saundra. His wife is white and Hawaiian Tropic out there certainly isn't that."

We left the sanctuary and returned to our table.

When our waiter came back with our drinks we noticed Brent and Hawaiian Tropic leaving in a hurry. A few seconds later the hostess came over to Asha and shoved a note in her hand.

Asha looked at me and back down at the balled up napkin. "What the hell?"

She silently passed the note over to me.

Neatly written in pink lipstick were the words STAY AWAY FROM BRENT OR ELSE.

Chapter 41

ASHA

The note surprised the hell out of us. Who would have expected that sweet-looking woman to be a closet Glenn Close? Saundra wanted to confront them before they got too far up the block but I didn't think that was the smart thing to do. Obviously Lula wasn't playing with a full deck and, if she was crazy enough to write the note, then who knew what else she was capable of. I didn't want to find out. Saundra suggested that I tell Brent that he might have a problem on his hands but I thought, why should I? He's a lying, cheating bastard and he should learn the hard way.

Kevin buzzed in that I had a phone call from you know who.

"Thanks, Kevin, I'll take it."

"This is Asha Mitchell."

A cleared throat. "Hey, Asha, it's Brent. How are you?"

"I'm fine and yourself?"

"Good, good. Hey, I just wanted to say . . ."

"One second, Brent, I got someone else on the line. Hold on."

I sat there with the phone on hold. I wanted him to suffer through this. After going to the water cooler down the hall and getting a Snickers out of the vending machine, I came back.

"Sorry about that, you were saying?"

"I was saying that I wanted to apologize about last night."

I rolled my eyes at how rehearsed his apology sounded. It's almost like he quantified the exact pitiful sounding tone and pitch to get my forgiveness.

"I don't know why you're apologizing, Brent. We have no commitment, so save that guilt trip for your wife."

Silence.

"Uh . . . okay. Well, then, can I see you tonight?"

"Sure."

A deep sigh of relief. "Good, I'll send a car to take you to the Four Seasons at about five-fifteen."

"Okay I'll see you then." I said calmly.

"*Ciao.*"

After work it was pouring rain and I ran to the sleek gray Lincoln Town Car and hopped in the backseat. The driver nodded a hello and took me to my destination. As I walked through the cold, geometrically complicated building and up the stairs to the discreet Four Seasons restaurant, all I kept thinking about was how I was going to bring up the ruby earrings.

"Good evening, Ms. Mitchell. How are you?" the maître d' asked.

"Fine, Lucio, and you?"

"Very well, *madame.* What is the name of your party and I'll check the list to see if they have arrived."

"Uh . . . Davis."

The maître d' squinted as he scanned the long list. "Ah, right this way please."

I was confused because there were no other Black people in the room. We stopped in front of a tall blonde sitting with her hands folded.

I tapped Lucio. "I'm sorry there has been some kind of mistake. I was looking for Mr. Brent Davis."

"There has been no mistake. I am *Mrs.* Brent Davis." The blonde said softly.

My heart began to thump wildly in my chest. Shit. What the hell was going on here? The tension must have been painfully obvious because Lucio scampered away like a frightened squirrel.

"Uh . . . hello . . . I'm . . ."

"I know who you are," she said with her eyes narrowing.

I couldn't believe this was happening. "What's this about, Mrs. Davis?"

Her mouth was drawn tightly in anger and when she parted her thinly glossed lips, it looked painful. "Please have a seat, Ms. Mitchell, we need to talk."

"I don't have anything to say to you, Mrs. Davis." I turned to walk away.

"If you take one more step, I will embarrass us both. Please sit down."

Now I was getting furious. A part of me wanted to test her but Mama always told me never to test someone who is desperate and has nothing to lose. I used the Four Seasons a lot for business and I couldn't afford to get banned. I eased down in the chair and sat there stoically.

"You have been sleeping with my husband for quite some time, Ms. Mitchell."

The turtleneck I was wearing felt like it was squeezing tighter and tighter around my throat. "Obviously if you went to this trouble to get me here, you must know for a fact that I am sleeping with Brent, so I won't insult your intelligence. But to be quite frank, Mrs. Davis, I think this is a personal problem between you and your husband."

Her milky skin became a rosacea-colored blush. She leaned forward with her teeth gritted. "I'm glad you won't insult my intelligence because I know exactly what you've been up to. I've been looking at all of Brent's receipts and credit card statements and the purchases . . ."

I held up my hand. "Like I said, this is between you and Brent. Don't worry about him seeing me anymore because I'm done with him. I don't need this drama."

She sat back with a smirk on her face. "It doesn't matter if you see him or not because I have filed for divorce and I'm going to take him for everything he has. So, Ms. Mitchell, he won't be able to afford Badgley Mishka and all those other gifts you've been receiving."

So much for the ruby earrings.

"How did you get me here?" I asked.

A waiter came over to take our order. He looked fresh from Sicily.

"I'll have a cup of Earl Grey," she said.

"I'll have the same."

She sat sideways so her long stockinged legs could cross. I could tell by her mannerisms that this woman came from old money.

"Brent was at home when he called you. I heard everything when he asked you to come here to meet him. I simply called his secretary back pretending to be you and cancelled so I could meet you here."

"I see."

She became even more relaxed and I did, too, for some reason. I guess it was because neither of us wanted anything to do with Brent anymore.

"Might I add, Ms. Mitchell, that it is to your credit that you are just as unapologetic about sleeping with my husband now as you were on the telephone."

This was getting too weird. "I think you've had your say, Mrs. Davis. I'm going to leave now." I stood up and grabbed my coat.

"You may leave now if you want to but I think you should know about Lula Karapachoo first."

"Who the hell is that?"

"My husband's other mistress, the Hawaiian that you met at Jade Crown."

"How did you know about the incident at the restaurant? Are you following me?" I asked, getting more and more angry.

She laughed and tossed her long hair behind her shoulder. "Of course not, I have better things to do. But I did hire a private investigator to follow Brent."

At that moment I pictured her producing shiny black-and-white photos of me giving her husband a blow job to show in court. "Oh, for Chrissakes," I said.

The waiter returned with the steaming hot tea. "May I have a Bacardi and Coke instead? I need a drink."

Annoyed, the waiter nodded crisply and removed the beverage.

"I don't know what to say, Mrs. Davis." I laughed at the sheer complexity of the situation. "So the note was a joke, then?"

She tilted her head in confusion. "What note?"

"When they left the restaurant, the hostess gave me a really weird note. It was rather threatening."

She shook her head as she sipped daintily from the teacup. "I certainly didn't tell her to write it but I'm not surprised."

"What do you mean?"

"Lula used to be my private eye. She dropped the case and refunded my money because she fell in love with Brent."

"You've gotta be joking."

A painful gaze transformed her beautiful face. "I wish I were."

"So how did she know I was going to be there with my sister?"

She shrugged. "That, I believe, was chance."

"I can't believe this. You hired her to watch Brent and she ended up sleeping with him?"

"That appears to be the situation. I suggest you be careful."

I drank two huge gulps from the Bacardi and Coke that had appeared in front of me.

"Sounds like we got a real live one here." I said.

"Pretty much."

"Well, I appreciate your warning me. I don't know if I would have done the same in your situation."

She didn't answer when I said good-bye.

The streets were slick and cars splashed water as they whizzed by but I didn't care. A man's wife just told one of her husband's mistresses to beware of the other mistress. That meant Lula must be pretty nutty. I clicked along in my heels for about ten blocks before I realized I might be in danger walking the streets, so I hailed a cab.

Saundra was already asleep on the sofa when I got home. I've told her a million time not to ruin my leather couch. Was she tired of sharing the bed with me? Well, that was just too bad.

It took me a while to get to sleep and, when I did, I still didn't rest. It was that right-below-the-surface sleep that might as well not be sleep at all because when you wake up you still feel tired.

Someone was knocking on my door. Frustated and groggy, I glanced toward the clock. Three o'clock in the morning!

"Who is it?" I asked.

"It's me. Saundra. The doorman just called. Brent wants to come up."

I thought about that Lula woman and I became suspicious.

"How do I know it's really him?"

"Asha, what are you talking about?"

I shook my head to clear it. There was no way I was going to add my drama to her already troubled mind. "Nothing. Let him come up."

I was surprised at how disheveled he looked when I opened the door. "What do you want, Brent?"

"I really need to talk to you. Please let me in."

"I don't think so."

"Please, Asha. I know about what happened at the Four Seasons. Amanda told me everything."

Saundra was staring at us both. She looked scared.

"Don't say another word, Brent, until we're in my room."

Once we were away from Saundra's distressed gaze, I faced him. "Why are you here?"

"I just had to clear things up after what happened between you and Amanda."

I sighed and flopped back. "Brent, none of that matters now. I'm through."

"No, Asha, please don't say that. I don't know what she told you but I'm sure it's not the truth."

I began to laugh but it wasn't as hearty as it would have been if I was well-rested and functioning. "Now why should I believe *you* that she lied to *me?*"

"She's not the one who filed for divorce, Asha. I'm the one who asked for it."

I felt my lips part in surprise. "Why?"

"I told her a few weeks ago that I wanted out because I fell in love with someone else."

I shook my head in disbelief. "Okay, whatever, but what does this all have to do with me?"

He reached in his pocket, pulled out a box and placed it on the bed between us. I opened it and a huge diamond ring sat nestled between the velvet slits. "I told Amanda that I'm leaving her so that I could marry you."

I looked at the glimmering diamond and back at Brent. Even if I did love him, which I didn't, I'd be a damn fool to marry a shameless adulterer.

"You've got to be joking."

Brent shook his head and got down on one knee. "Asha . . ."

"Brent get up off the damn floor, take this ring and go home," I said.

"I know what you're thinking . . . that I'd cheat on you like I did with Amanda."

I sat looking at him in utter disbelief. "Brent, I don't love you and I have never loved you. When we first hooked up, I told you that I had plans never to commit to anybody. I thought we were cool *because* you were married. And now that you're getting a divorce you think you love me?"

Brent sat back down. "I don't believe you don't want to be with me."

This pompous bastard. He thinks he is such a catch that it's impossible that I wouldn't want him.

It was definitely time for him to go. "Why do you want a black wife now, anyway?"

"I was young and ambitious. Amanda just went along with the package."

I respected him even less. "So you never loved her?"

He got up. "I just liked how she looked on my arm but I never stopped loving the sisters."

I folded my arms. "No, you mean you never stopped *fucking* the sisters."

Brent smiled and slipped on his coat. "You are one tough nut to crack, girl, you know that?"

"Yup."

Brent snapped the ring box shut. "I got someone else anyway who'll appreciate this ring a whole lot more."

"Lula? Good. You and that psycho bitch deserve each other."

"What are you talking about?"

"Lula is a private investigator. Amanda hired her to keep tabs on you and then she fell in love."

His eyes were practically popping out of his head. "What?"

"Yup! She fell in love with you and refunded Amanda's money."

He just sat there, frozen with shock.

"Get out, Brent, and please make sure you tell Lula that we broke up tonight. I don't want her harassing me."

He looked like he was going to say something else but then he just smiled. "Good-bye, Asha Mitchell."

"Good-bye, Brent."

He stood in front of me with his arms outstretched. "Aren't you gonna give me a hug?"

I shook my head. "Nah, that's all right."

His smile faded and I walked him to the door.

As soon as Brent was gone, it hit me. I was now responsible for my own rent and other basic bills. On top of that, I was feeding and housing my sister.

Something had to give.

Chapter 42

SAUNDRA

I'm going to pieces. My fiancée doesn't try to contact me anymore. My father is a closet homosexual. Evelyn will never be my stepmother. Asha and I are going to be murdered one of these days by one of the men or women that she is playing games with. I can't go back to Queens and I have no money of my own to escape Asha's dangerous crazy house. I feel like I have no foundation, no anchor. I'm just free floating from day to day and it will be at least another month before school starts again. What do I do in the meantime?

I felt like calling Yero. Maybe he could help me figure out what my next step should be.

But I can't talk to Yero because he will only have one thing on his mind: Getting back together. And I'm in no shape to be in a relationship.

I'm on my own. A solitary figure walking the streets of downtown Manhattan in the frigid weather with my hat pulled low on my forehead, my gloved hands shoved deep into my coat pockets.

I ambled on. Up one street and down another.

I peered from beneath the hat and saw homeless men and women shivering on the sidewalk, a piece of cardboard their only defense against the icy wind. I saw the drug dealers, their eyes shifting from side to side because they had to make on-the-spot decisions—a prospective buyer was either a junkie or a cop. The wrong decision could cost them twenty years of freedom under New York State's stiff drug laws.

I saw fear in the eyes of the working poor and anger in the pupils of the unemployed.

In the beginning I believed that walking would release some precious endorphins that would act as a balm on my wounds but that didn't happen.

Who was this new Saundra and what were her new goals now that Yero was gone?

Chapter 43

ASHA

The shower was running and I heard Nick singing that old song "Give It To Me Baby" by Rick James. It was funny hearing him imitate Rick's voice and the bass line a capella, but then it hit me. Someone he called Baby Girl was in love with him back in Houston and he was here with me without guilt or shame. She was probably somewhere in her bedroom thinking about him with little hearts dancing around her head.

Between Saundra and Yero and Brent and Amanda and Lula, my deceit cup had runneth over.

"Give It To Me Baby" morphed into "Ghetto Life" in Nick's shower medley.

I opened the bathroom door. A cloud of hot steam was the only air. Nick peeked out of the shower curtain and smiled when he saw me.

"You wanna lather me up?" He began moving his body from side to side so his dick slapped both thighs. It was hilarious.

"No."

He frowned. "So why did you let that cold air in?"

"I need to talk to you."

"It couldn't wait until I finished washing?"

I watched him lather up with just a bar of soap and wondered why he didn't use a washcloth.

"No, it can't wait."

"Well?"

I was about to change my mind because Baby Girl was an adult and should handle her own business but I was emotionally exhausted. "Tell Baby Girl that you date other people."

Nick stopped washing. "Say what?"

"You heard me."

"Why?"

"Because it's the right thing to do."

"Whoa. Don't tell me that you have grown a conscience?"

I laughed and went to the kitchen to order some coconut rice and basil shrimp from the Thai restaurant.

Nick came out with my white Ralph Lauren towel wrapped around his waist. He looked damn good. "Now, what's this nonsense all about?"

"Do you want Thai food?"

"I don't want no Chinese food."

"It's Thai not Chinese, Nick."

He sucked his teeth. "All of it is the same. I'd rather have a tortilla." He started snapping his fingers and saying, "Olé!"

I cancelled the Thai food and ordered Mexican takeout for both of us.

He kissed me on the cheek. "I'm gonna go get dressed."

Gonzalez and Gonzalez came fast.

"Nick your food is here."

"I'll be done in a second."

He took longer to get dressed than any woman I know. Everything had to be perfect.

But he sure looked good when he stepped out of that room. It made me want to go back to bed but Saundra had discreetly left us alone to go to the movies. That meant two hours. She would be home any second.

"If I didn't know better, I'd swear you were gay," I teased him.

"Watch it, Asha. Just 'cause a man likes to take care of himself and wear nice clothes doesn't mean he has sugar in his tank."

"Sorry about that."

"Besides, gay men are cool."

"Why are gay men cool, Nick?"

"Don't you get it? In the jungle the key to survival is less competition among predators. Gay men are cool because there's more pussy for me. That's why I don't understand cats that be hatin' on them, dumb muthafuckas don't know that gays make it easier for us!"

I couldn't believe I was in some kind of zone and actually listening to his ridiculous little ghetto philosophy. "Are you still mentoring that kid?"

"No. He dropped out of the program. I'm getting another one in the spring, though."

"Well, could you please stop the thug talk? It is truly tired."

He looked down in the Mexican food bag. "You're absolutely right, Asha. Do you believe they didn't send any sour cream?"

I opened the greasy bag and emptied its contents on the coffee table. "Nope, all they put in here is salt, pepper, and ketchup."

"I can't eat a tortilla without sour cream."

"I think there might be some in the fridge."

Nick dumped almost the whole cup of sour cream on that tortilla.

"That's disgusting."

"Don't worry about my food."

I put my food on my black Crate and Barrel plate and sat down next to Nick.

"So why you want me to take a bullet from Baby Girl?" he asked.

"I just don't feel comfortable knowing she is pinning her hopes on an illusion. If she still wants to roll with you after the talk, then that's on her."

He shook his head. "Saundra's rubbing off on you, girl. Meditation isn't far behind."

"It's not like that."

"Yes it is, and that's a good thing."

"Stop it."

"I'll drop Baby Girl and all the rest of my women if you'll give me a real chance."

I resisted the smile tugging at my lips. "What is a real chance?"

Nick stopped moving around and his expression became very serious. He spoke slowly and distinctly. "We both stop seeing other people."

"Maybe."

"Wow! Are you serious?"

"Maybe."

"Then maybe I'll talk to Baby Girl and maybe I won't."

"I really need to think about it, Nick."

"We've known each other for four years and been hitting the sheets for the past twelve months and you still need more thinking time?" He stopped eating and pushed the food away. "I don't want any more of this."

He was getting mad and I needed to chill him out. "Just twenty-four more hours."

Nick's eyes were cold. "Why?"

The truth was I'm just plain commitment phobic but he was in no mood to hear anything like that so I shifted the blame to my sister. "I need to give you 100 percent, Nick. After all this time you don't deserve any less, but most of the time I'm wondering what really happened to Saundra or how to get her back with Yero or should I give up the apartment. Stuff like that."

"And how are you going to solve all that in twenty-four hours?"

I massaged his shoulders and kissed his neck. "I don't want to lose you. I just said that to buy some time."

He started kissing me back. "Just say you're my woman and we'll solve your problems together."

It was the moment of truth and I knew that if he walked out that door, we were over.

"I'm your woman," I whispered softly.

Nick grinned like he'd hit the Lotto and it made me feel better than I had in weeks.

Chapter 44

SAUNDRA

Asha had been humming and singing to herself for the past two days and that could only mean one thing. She had a new man in her life. Ever since the situation with Brent and his wife, I had been living in fear that Asha's lifestyle was going to get me killed. The fear made me realize that I wanted to live and worked to give me new energy. Who was this new guy? Was he married? Did he make a living doing something legal? I had to know. So, one morning after Asha left for work, I violated her right to privacy.

There was nothing noteworthy in her bathroom cabinet—cold cream, Midol, aspirin, diet pills, rubbing alcohol and throat lozenges.

In the bedroom, I sorted through her desk drawers. The cancelled checks told me that Asha paid her rent, cable, electricity and phone bills on time, which was surprising. Her bank statements showed electronic deposits of her paycheck plus a regular sum of money that made me gasp. Where on earth did Asha get $10,000 on the first of every month to put in her bank account? I riffled through those papers, my heart beating fast. Was she a mule for some drug dealer? I learned that she had started receiving the money exactly twelve months before which meant that she had somehow gotten her hands on $120,000 and it wasn't through her work as an accessories buyer. Why? How? I would just have to confront her about it and take my punishment for snooping. If I could somehow stop Asha from doing whatever it was and possibly save her life, the anger that she would unleash on me for snooping would be a small price to pay.

I shut the drawer and shifted my attention to the boxes on the top shelf of her closet.

The smallest one was the size of a shoebox. It was crammed with naked pictures of Nick Seabrook. Standing. Sitting. Lying on one side. Lying on another side. Up against the kitchen wall. In the shower. Standing on the edge of the tub. On a beach. In a car. On a car. Jesus!

My fingers shook as I flipped the latch on a large, floral decorated container. There were dozens and dozens of letters. The outside envelopes were addressed from Roger Mitchell to Lola Smith and the postmarks told me that Mama had received them from Asha's father when they were both just teenagers. I was tempted to read them but were the young thoughts of Roger Mitchell any of my business? Asha obviously didn't think so because she'd never mentioned this treasure to me.

It was all so unfair, I thought as I left Asha's bedroom. It was wrong that Roger had been either unable or unwilling to fight whatever demons that had led him to the crack pipe. It was terrible that Mama's weakness for Roger had led her to stay in that relationship until it damaged her spirit. It was despicable of Philip to use Mama's body to try to figure out whether he liked men or women and then leave her with another baby to take care of. It was unfair to both me and Asha that Mama worried so much, ate so much, drank so much that she finally keeled over from a stroke before we had a chance to figure out a path for our own lives.

Chapter 45

ASHA

When Mr. Delrossi took his seat at the conference room table, I tapped my water glass for order. Several of the senior staff, my associate buyer, and our guests turned to look at me.

Tucked firmly in my Ann Taylor skirt suit and wearing pearls, I said, "Thank you all for stopping by to meet Splash Brady and Reena Sendo who are partners in Splash Sendo, a brand-new two-woman firm that manufacturers a line of the cutest little handbags to hit the scene since Kate Spade."

I took a breather and looked at the two perky blondes, barely out of their teens, whom I was talking about. Splash was the trendy girlfriend of an Emmy Award–winning actor and Reena was a party girl about town who seemed to get a truckload of media attention just for walking down the street. Both of them seemed very sullen considering the fact that I had recently ordered $100,000 worth of merchandise from Splash Sendo.

Splash tossed a sheaf of her thick, waist-length hair back over her shoulder and looked down at her hands.

Reena gave her partner an angry glare and managed a tight smile of thanks.

The only thing I could do was ignore the tension between them and keep going.

"We're here to talk about shipping dates, store selections, and cross-promotional opportunities," I said enthusiastically. "Splash, why don't you start with some of your ideas?"

"Let Reena do it. She knows everything," Splash hissed out of the corner of her mouth.

Something was terribly wrong.

"Sure," Reena said. "Our market is the hip, downtown New York crowd and young people across the country who want to look like them. We think that five-minute commercials before the start of the hit teen movies will catch their attention. In the meantime, Splash and I will . . ."

Splash snorted in a very unladylike way before Reena could finish her sentence. "Probably kill each other."

Reena flushed and ignored the comment. "Splash and I will use our connections to hit the talk show circuit, always carrying one of the bags on camera."

"The only connections you have are your tits," Splash said loud enough for everyone at the table to hear.

I had to do something. "Perhaps this isn't a good day for you ladies. Let's reschedule this meeting for a time when you're under less pressure."

Reena closed her eyes.

Splash looked triumphant.

Delrossi harrumphed and asked me, "Ms. Mitchell, how far are we along in this venture?"

"Sir, we've ordered more than one gross. This seems to be a minor glitch. Please don't worry about it."

Splash hit the table with her fist. "The *Titanic* was a minor glitch compared to what my double-crossing partner has done to my relationship."

So this was about a man. I knew right then that the handbag line was over and, unless our legal department could get our deposit back quickly, so was my job.

Mr. Delrossi was staring at me. His eyebrows were raised. Not a good sign.

"Meeting over," I announced.

Splash and Reena stood along with the rest of the staff.

I halted their departure with a raise of my hand. "Not you two.

There are legal issues here that must be worked out. Don't you dare move."

Reena sighed loudly.

Splash sat back down, too, but she clearly didn't give a fuck about whatever was going to happen to her.

That meant Reena had won the man and Splash was in full self-destructive mode as a result.

Chapter 46

SAUNDRA

If Asha had not been my sister, I would have just taken my things and become another camper in Yero's already overcrowded house, but if she was headed for trouble, I needed to try to stop her. I planned to find out what the deal was with this new guy by starting a friendly sort of girlfriend-to-girlfriend conversation and making her feel comfortable enough to tell me.

It didn't work out that way.

I had spent the day checking out various museum exhibits around the city and came home to chaos. When I opened the door the first thing I saw was a pair of pink panties lying right in the middle of the floor. An empty liquor bottle wasn't too far away and the line of clothing—including men's boxer shorts, a man's shirt and pants—led straight to Asha's bedroom door, which was wide open.

I looked in, expecting to see Nick, but the guy was much shorter and his head was completely bald. They were both sound asleep and the smell of liquor rose and fell from their open mouths, creating a disgusting stench.

Should I have just closed the door and gone on about my business? Yes. Did I? No.

I shook my sister's bare shoulder until her eyes opened. "Asha! Who on earth is this guy? What are you doing?"

Asha sat up with tits hanging and bush showing. She rubbed her eyes, yawned and squinted her eyes at me. "What did you say?"

I repeated my questions.

Asha turned around and looked at her playmate. "Just some guy I met in a bar. Could you get me some water? Jesus, my head is killing me."

"Some guy you met in a bar? How do you know he's not a serial killer? Wake him up and get him out of here!"

She held her head in her hands, groaned and then ran bare-assed into the bathroom. I could hear her retching.

By the time she pulled on a robe and stumbled into the kitchen, I was sitting there at the table wondering if this was the first time Asha had done something so incredibly hazardous.

"Asha, have you lost your mind?"

"Leave me alone, Saundra. In fact, get out. You're on my last goddamn nerve."

She was clearly still drunk so I wasn't too hurt.

She filled a glass with water from the tap and drank it down too quickly. This caused her to throw up all over the floor. "What was that rat of yours doing out of its cage?"

"My hamster?"

Asha used some paper towels to clean up her mess.

"I came home and it was running wild. That so-called serial killer was nice enough to catch it. All these animals have got to go. First thing in the morning."

What had happened to my life? What would become of me? "Shut up!" I screamed. "Just shut up you fucking two-bit tramp!"

Asha's robe flew open as she lunged at me. "How dare you judge me? Who gave you the right to do that?"

Before things could get any worse, the man appeared. He looked both scared and hungover. "I've got to go."

He looked at me and held out a hand. "Hi, I'm Clark."

I ignored his outstretched hand.

As we watched, Clark picked up his clothes, piece by piece, and disappeared. We heard the bathroom door close.

I hugged my sister's half-clad body. "I'm sorry. What's the matter, Asha? Why did you do something like this?"

She pulled away. "My boss is on my ass because I might have cost the store a whole lot of money fucking around with two stupid bitches who let an argument over a man get in the way of business. I'm afraid to go into my own living room because you have it cluttered up with scary looking statues, weird-sounding music and more creatures than fucking Doctor Doolittle. On top of that, I want to know what happened with Phil and you won't tell me."

I shook my head. "No. I won't talk about Phil. I can't. And don't make that an excuse for bringing a total stranger into our home. It was dangerous, Asha. In fact, he is still here so we're not in the clear yet."

We were still yelling and screaming at each other when Clark left, closing the front door behind himself without saying another word.

Chapter 47

ASHA

I don't see this working. As a matter of fact, I know my new living situation is not going to work.

Our fight was not about run-of-the-mill sister stuff—stop eating all the chocolate or don't wear my silk blouse.

Those types of rifts can be repaired. No, the blow up between me and Saundra was big enough to drive a truck through.

True, bringing that guy home from happy hour was stupid. I've never done anything like that before but that day I had been thinking about myself as Nick's woman. Some man's woman. Something owned. Someone who was going to be betrayed. I flipped!

On top of that, I lost out on a job promotion over the Splash Sendo mess. The two bickering partners returned our money but the whole incident hurt my credibility.

But getting back to Saundra. I knew the very second I opened that door that me and Saundra were not designed to be room-mates. Why didn't I just call Yero to come fix this shit and take her over to his house?

Saundra is not a bad person.

She is the kind of woman who most people don't ever get the chance to meet—kind, gentle, faithful, spiritual, non-materialistic, honest to a fault with a genuine love for all of mankind.

When Mama died, she made sure that Phil understood we were always going to be sisters. There was not going to be any of that "time and distance caused Asha and Saundra to drift apart" crap. Saundra made Phil agree to let her call and come see me whenever and however she wanted. She told me all that the week after Mama's funeral and I've never loved her more than I did at that moment.

So, my question is: How do you get rid of a younger sister who is driving you crazy but doesn't deserve to be thrown out?

Before the Clark incident, Saundra would have said that her moving in with me had made our bond stronger than ever. And I would have grudgingly acknowledged that I was relieved she had me to turn to during her dark night of the soul.

But if she keeps preaching at me, I'm going to explode. After the dust settles, our relationship will be in microscopic pieces. We'll end up parting company, never to call or speak to each other again.

In the meantime, I'm going to avoid her as much as possible. This shit just ain't working.

Chapter 48

SAUNDRA

Asha got dumped in high school and she changed. Mom died and she changed. My father bought a house a few years ago and I moved in and she changed. Now I need to stay with her for a while and she has changed again. I am so sick and tired of Asha and her changes. If she changed for the better that would be one thing, but anytime she gets the slightest disappointment or inconvenience, she expects the world to care; and when it doesn't, she gets more and more withdrawn or just plain mean. She actually had the nerve to say "you should have known better than to trust Phil or get engaged because none of that fairy tale shit ever works." What kind of thing is that to say when your sister's life has been shattered? Not cool at all.

I always suspected that Asha was jealous of my relationship with my father because her father was such a deadbeat; and now I'm sure that she would laugh at me about how Phil really turned out. Acting against God, that's how he turned out. Asha's dad was a tormented drug addict but at least he liked women. I simply can't stand the idea of Asha's secret mocking and ridicule. That is why I have not been able to tell her the truth about Phil.

Her dad was nothing but a drug addict and he never so much as gave Mama a penny to help raise her. My father gave more than his fair share to Mama after they broke up. They were together for a few months after I was born but Daddy said she dumped him because she never truly got over Asha's crappy father. Mom would never talk about why she broke up with my dad and I always assumed she didn't because she knew she really blew it by tossing back such a great catch. I vowed to myself I would never make that mistake if I met the right man, and that's why I took a chance with Yero.

Well, I was wrong about my own father but I'll never let Asha know just how wrong. She won't have me to kick around much longer. I'm quitting school, getting a job and my own place even if it is just a room no bigger than a cell. After that, we'll never have to see or speak to each other again.

Chapter 49

PHIL

Ihad a concussion.

I didn't want to hurt Evelyn any further by telling the emergency room doctors what really happened, so I told them and the police department that I slipped and fell in my own driveway. After a two-night stay in the hospital, I signed myself out and went back to work. With zero tolerance for lying suspects or anyone who resisted my attempts to put the cuffs on, I worked double shifts to the point of exhaustion. My weight was dropping, Hugo and I were barely speaking, and out on the street the words "excessive force" were being linked with my name. But I didn't care. I realized that I really did love Evelyn. Not in that man/woman way that she needed but like a best friend or beloved sister. What I hadn't known for all this time was that I depended on Evelyn and she had become my rock, my foundation. Losing her really hurt. Knowing that she hated me was as unbearable as losing Saundra. That's why Hugo and I were on the outs. He could not understand my grief over Evelyn. Worse, he refused to go visit her and apologize for his role in her tragedy. And he really needed to do that, because the whole Evelyn as decoy thing had been his idea.

I was twenty-one years old when I became a cop and scared to death that someone on the force would find out that I was gay.

So, I stopped dating altogether and for the next four years, I used work to ease my loneliness and misery. When Lola started coming on to me, I resisted at first. Then I began to imagine how wonderful it would be if I could really make it with a woman. No more sneaking and hiding—I could go back and reunite with Mom and Dad, see how my little brothers had turned out, and have a "normal life." So I started going downstairs to see Lola and her little girl, Asha. What a cute kid! It felt good to put money in Lola's hand and know that she was going to buy some nice clothes for Asha or a new pair of shoes for herself. Lola was a good woman—funny, kind, warm. She just wasn't what I needed and, since I didn't tell her the truth, she blamed herself. She accused me of thinking she was too ugly, too fat, too yellow, too poor. It drove me crazy. One night I gave her what she wanted. Saundra was born nine months later.

I felt awful when Lola told me she was pregnant. She was already struggling with one child and there was no way I could marry her. I watched her deteriorate emotionally and vowed to leave women alone forever.

Then I met Hugo. He had a reputation around the station house as this Latino heartthrob who had a string of ladies, but it takes a gay man to know a gay man. I peeped his card right away and he knew it.

We'd been doing our thing for a month or two when he scared the hell out of me. People in the precinct were talking, he said. Wondering why the two of us were always together. Why I didn't seem to have a woman. Hugo said he had an idea. His old friend, Evelyn, was divorced, lived at home with her elderly mother and needed a man to take her out from time to time. What was the harm? he asked. The other cops would get hip to my new "girlfriend" and stop the talk. Evelyn would have a social life until she met someone else, and everybody would be happy.

I bought it.

Then Lola died and that changed everything. I had to take Saundra or let her go into foster care and what did I know about mothering a grieving teenage girl? She was the only biological family I had left and there was no way I was going to lose her to drugs or one of these knuckleheads out here who just wanted to get in her panties. Evelyn was just what the doctor ordered. But I wasn't crazy. I wanted Evelyn to take over Lola's job and make sure that Saundra turned into a decent, educated, sensible woman who had clear goals and didn't sleep around. Evelyn wanted a lover. Plain and simple. Only very small children or simple-minded adults expect to get their needs met without giving the other person what they want.

So I became Evelyn's sexual partner. At first Hugo was furious and threatened to tell Evelyn the truth. I told him that I'd shoot him in the balls, cut him off for life and simply find another Evelyn to mother Saundra. Only this time it would be a woman who he didn't know.

Evelyn's long-term feelings didn't enter into the plan at all.

Looking back, it was a diabolical plot and it would serve me right if Evelyn emptied every bullet out of her gun into my heart.

I miss Saundra but she won't return my calls and I'm not putting my business on paper, so sending a letter is out of the question. A whole lot of people are in jail right now because they like writing letters—letters of apology, letters of confession, letters of need, want, hate.

Sometimes, I sit across the street from Asha's apartment building in an unmarked car watching Saundra go in and out. I've thought about just walking up to her and demanding that she hear me out but I don't have the right to make any demands of her.

I decided to go through Asha. She agreed to meet with me but insisted that Yero join us too. At first I said no. I mean, who wants to discuss this type of shit with another man at the table. When I said no, Asha hung up the phone without another word. So now we're doing this her way.

I had to laugh when she laid out her terms: The meeting was to take place at some restaurant in Manhattan and dinner plus drinks were on me. I got there fifteen minutes early, scoped out the place and took a seat way in the back near the kitchen door.

No-man's land. Far from the other customers who would not be able to overhear our conversation.

She glided in wearing a pants suit that probably cost more than I made in a month. The woman was the spitting image of her mother—physically that is. Their personalities could not have been more different. If Lola had had even a quarter of Asha's self-confidence and bring-it-straight-or-don't-bring-it-at-all braggadocio, she would be alive today. And Yero . . . he looked lost.

"How are y'all doing?" I asked after they sat down.

They both just glowered at me, saying nothing.

I motioned toward a waitress.

"Is anybody drinking?"

"I don't want anything to eat or drink," Yero said crisply. "Just tell me what happened between you and Saundra. Then I'm outta here."

Asha picked up a menu. "I'll have a cosmopolitan. Also the French onion soup."

It was all I could do not to smile. Asha would always be primarily about Asha.

I knew that if I had a drink of anything alcoholic, the meeting would turn into a disaster. Yero clearly wanted to take a swing at me and if I wasn't a cop, he would have done it already. Sober, I was willing to take one punch. Drunk, I would hurt the poor boy.

"I'll have a ginger ale and a steak, well done, with the rice pilaf." I said.

We all stared at each other.

"Talk man," Yero growled.

"Okay, but I need you to hear me out. From beginning to end. I'm about to go way back. To a place called Dayton, Ohio."

They looked at each other and then back at me.

I took a deep breath and started with the story of Willie, the little boy I liked in the first grade.

By the time the food arrived, I was telling them both about my early days in New York, right before I took the police exam.

Asha looked shocked. I couldn't read Yero's expression.

When the waitress left, I threw my hands up in exasperation. "Will one of y'all say something?"

"What does all this have to do with Saundra?" Yero asked.

There was nothing to do but continue. By the time I got to the part where Saundra walked in on me and Hugo, the steak in front of me was cold. Asha had downed two more drinks and Yero's expression had softened.

"And now I've lost the only family I had left."

Yero shook his head. "Saundra still loves you, man. She just had you up on a pedestal and you fell off. It's a shame that it had to come out like that. You should have told her the truth a long time ago. In fact, she should have grown up knowing the truth about you."

Asha shook her head. "I just cannot believe that I've been through all this bullshit just because you and Hugo turned out to be gay. It's unbelievable! Saundra's supposed to be all about people accepting each other for who they are. She's supposed to be Miss Peace and Love! To tell you the truth, I feel like kicking her crybaby ass. What a hypocrite!"

"Ah, the sounds of compassion," I said dryly.

Asha wiped her mouth and pushed back her chair. "That's real fucked up what you did to Evelyn, man. I'll save my compassion for her."

"So what now?" I asked.

Asha's voice dripped with contempt. "You broke Saundra's heart but you won't ruin her life. I have to get Yero and Saundra together and put this wedding back on track. You go back to Hugo and do whatever you were doing. I'm leaving."

I watched them walk away, hoping that someone would find some forgiveness in their heart. It would be nice to watch Saundra get married.

Chapter 50

ASHA

Saundra didn't want to hear Phil's story but I made her ass sit still and listen. She didn't comment on any of it but a few days later, she approached me and apologized for anything she had done to offend me. I was cool with that. Then she said that we were too different to live under the same roof and make it work. I silently agreed with that. But when she hit me with the news that she wasn't going back to school, that she was going to get a job and her own place, something had to be done.

I called Yero and told him that I'd be in Houston with Nick on Christmas day and that he should come over and talk some sense into Saundra.

"She'll tell the doorman that I can't come up," he answered miserably.

What a wuss. A nice, hardworking guy. But still a wuss.

"Yero, pay attention. Every woman wants to be with her lover on the major holidays. When a woman is alone on Valentine's Day, Christmas, or New Year's Eve, her biggest fantasy is that the man she cares about will ring that bell and take her in his arms. It usually only happens in the movies but you need to man up and go get your woman back."

"Man up?" he bristled. "*She* dumped *me!*"

I couldn't help sighing. "Yero, do you want to debate me or marry Saundra?"

"Marry Saundra," he muttered.

"Then shut up and listen. Buy her a present, preferably jewelry. Buy her some candy and flowers. Bring all that good shit and yourself to my apartment on Christmas morning."

"What if you're wrong and I just make a fool of myself in front of the doorman again?"

My patience was wearing thin. This guy had no imagination at all. But then, neither did Saundra. These two definitely deserved each other. "Meet me in front of Madison Square Garden tomorrow morning at nine o'clock. I'm going to loan you my house keys. I'll explain the situation to the doorman so that if Saundra says no, you can go on up anyway. But I promise you that she'll open that door."

Chapter 51

SAUNDRA

Christmas Day was unseasonably warm. After an unsuccessful attempt at meditation and with no animals to play with, I turned on the news and heard that it was an astonishing sixty degrees outside. I decided to stay in my nightgown for the whole day. What was the point of showering? Why bother to get dressed? No company was coming over and I didn't even plan to answer the phone for fear of having to hang up on Phil. I figured that poor Evelyn was even more miserable than I was.

I was watching *The Honeymooners* marathon and eating celery sticks when the doorman buzzed.

"There's a Yero Brown here to see you, miss."

I didn't hesitate for a second. "Send him up, please."

It had been far too long since I'd seen my honey. Without thinking, I flew out of the apartment and stood in front of the elevator. The door opened and there he stood.

He looked beaten, shocked, and grief-stricken.

"Yero!"

A smile spread across his brown face and the light reentered his eyes. "Saundra!"

In less than a second, he was holding me, two packages and a bouquet of flowers in his arms. "Baby, baby."

His lips covered mine before I could answer. We hugged and kissed for what seemed like eternity.

"Why did you leave me?" Yero asked.

"Because I was a fool."

He waited for more.

I wrung my hands. "I don't know how to say it . . . Phil . . . he . . ."

Yero held my hands. "I know the whole story. I'm so sorry about that, baby. But why didn't you come to me? Why Asha?"

"She's my sister."

Yero sighed. "I still love you, Saundra."

I put my arms around his waist. "Yero, I'm sorry."

He nuzzled my hair with his chin. "I need more, honey. We both have to understand our breakup and why my shoulder wasn't the one you chose to cry on."

"You're right."

"Saundra," he whispered.

"What?"

"Will you marry me?"

My body felt weightless and when our lips met again, it felt like we were floating on a cloud.

We kissed until someone got off another elevator and stared at me, standing there all rumpled and still in my nightgown.

My hand flew to my mouth. "Yero, I've locked us out of the apartment."

He winked and grabbed me by the hand. "Don't worry, Asha gave me the key."

Chapter 52

PHIL

For six months I prayed that Saundra would bend, just a little. And then one morning I reached into the mailbox and there was only one pale pink envelope in it—an invitation to her wedding. I literally screamed with joy.

That same day me and my new partner, a good white cop named Andy Byer, with ten years under his belt, were rolling down Guy Brewer Boulevard. We were on our way to check out a tip about a new crystal meth ring that was operating in South Jamaica when we saw this kid run out of a store with an armful of clothes. Since we were traveling in an unmarked car, he didn't think twice about dashing right in front of us. The kid was black. The man who came tearing out the store after him was Middle Eastern.

Andy sighed in disgust.

I knew just what he meant. We had to stop the robbery that was going on right under our noses, but then this pissant one-hundred-dollar case would tie us up in paperwork for half the afternoon.

We got out and did our thing. The store owner ended up with his gear back. The kid was cuffed in the back of our car.

Andy started the car up and we were back in business. As we

rolled along, I turned around and stared hard into our prisoner's eyes.

"How old are you, man?"

He tried to look tough but I saw the fear in his eyes. "Twelve."

"Have you ever been arrested before?"

"No."

"Ever been in a police station?"

"No."

I couldn't help the groan that escaped. This was one of the happiest days of my life and the last thing I felt like doing was throwing a brand new baby into the maws of the criminal justice system.

"What's your name?"

"Hot Sauce."

"Boy, I know damned well your mother didn't name you Hot Sauce. Now cut the bad-ass act. I want your real name, not some dumb shit they call you in the street."

"Dennis Clark."

I spoke over my shoulder. "Hey, Andy! Give me a pen and paper."

He complied.

"Now, Dennis Clark, give me your address and phone number."

He rattled off the information and I turned back around. "Stop the car!" I yelled at Andy.

My partner pulled over.

I got out of the car and opened the back door. When I reached for little Dennis "Hot Sauce" Clark, I truly thought he was going to faint. The little wannabe thug figured he was about to become a victim of police brutality.

"Dennis, I'm going to take the cuffs off and let you go, but I'm going to keep an eye on you for the next couple of months and if you even breathe wrong, the cuffs go back on. Now, who do you live with?"

"My mother and my brother."

I let him go with a stern warning and prayed that he had been scared enough to stay out of trouble.

In the meantime, I just wanted to think about my daughter.

My unrelenting grief over the end of my relationship with both Saundra and Evelyn had caused Hugo and me to break up for good. Funny thing is, I didn't miss him. Had all that sneaking around created and sustained a false passion between us? I didn't spend too much time thinking about it after the invitation arrived. That pink envelope meant that I had another chance to be the honest, courageous man that my daughter had always believed me to be. It meant that the door might not be open, but it had cracked a little and I was willing to work long and hard to get it all the way open.

Chapter 53

SAUNDRA

On a hot summer day, I came out of Asha's bedroom dressed in my A-line, satin wedding gown, which had a top layer of soft netting adorned with hand sewn seed pearls. Asha walked behind me carrying the train, which she then helped me wrap around one arm.

Nick whistled softly. "You look gorgeous, Saundra." And he kissed me on the cheek.

"I still have to pin her hair up and hook the tiara into it," Asha said. "But she really is a stunning bride."

An hour later, I had allowed Asha to talk me into wearing lipstick and it was time to go. Asha and Nick were my attendants and we were riding in a white Rolls Royce. Later on, that same car would take me and my husband to the airport—we were going to honeymoon in Bermuda.

Asha is the greatest sister in the world. After I stopped speaking to Phil, we still had the Crystal Palace, which he and Hugo had paid for. But there was practically no money to pay for all the extras—dress, cake, cars, satin shoes and all the other niceties that I didn't know I wanted until Asha dangled them in front of my nose. Asha paid for everything except the rings. The ring bills belonged to Yero.

I wondered if Phil had received the invitation and whether he would show up. In my own way, I tried not to care but it was hard to erase all the good that he had done. Yes, he should have told me a long time ago that he was gay and he certainly should not have deceived Evelyn. But on the issue of good fathering, there was no question that Phil was the best.

I told Yero that if Phil showed up, I would ask him to walk me down the aisle.

We reached Central Park a half hour late. A large group of Mama's relatives and Yero's relatives was waiting for my arrival. In the middle of it all was Daddy, taking pictures of everything and everybody in sight.

It was so good to see him!

He opened the door before my driver could get out of the car. I smiled up at him and tears filled his eyes as he held out a hand to help me.

Chapter 54

ASHA

Why did Saundra go around digging up all of Mama's broke-ass, un-known relatives I wondered as I watched a bunch of women with their hair done up in gelled-to-the-max ghetto sculptures. They heaped pasta and chicken on the little appetizer plates like we weren't going to have a formal sit-down dinner in an hour. One of them was even stuffing fried shrimp in a paper bag that must have been bought for that purpose. Of course they were all loud and soon they were drunk. They'd better enjoy the hell out of themselves because Nick and I are getting married next sum-mer and you can bet your last dollar that these seafood-stealing bitches will not be on the scene. The Seabrook family is already having a fit because he gave me an engagement ring. Seeing this bunch would just kill Nick's mother outright. And why should I feel guilty? Mama's family left us to fend for ourselves after she died.

Saundra and Yero are grinning like they hit the lottery and, yes, I had a lump in my throat during their first dance because this day had come so close to not happening. That would have been a tragedy because they love each other so very, very much. When Phil led Saundra out on the floor for the father/daughter waltz, I actually did cry and Nick dabbed at his eyes, too.

I wonder how Evelyn is doing. I know that up until the last

minute, Saundra was hoping she would show up. I wanted that to happen also for Saundra's sake. But no one can blame the sister for putting Phil, Saundra, and the whole mess behind her. I just hope she didn't have a nervous breakdown or something.

If I had a magic wand, I would wave it around and make Phil a straight up heterosexual and Evelyn would suddenly appear on his arm. They would raise their champagne glasses along with the rest of us to toast Saundra and Yero. But I don't have one so all I can do is fold myself into Nick's arms, let him lead me onto the floor for our own dance, and pray that our wedding day is as lovely as this one.

A CONVERSATION WITH ANITA DOREEN DIGGS

Q. Evelyn Blake is the unsung heroine of this story. Who or what was your inspiration for this character?

A. I didn't have a specific person in mind. She just represents an updated version of the thousands of black women who have made tremendous sacrifices to finish raising children who were not their own.

Q. What would Lola Smith say to Evelyn if she could?

A. These two women were certainly too dissimilar to ever become friends or even have more than a short conversation with each other. However, whatever her other failings, Lola did have good manners. She would look Evelyn straight in the eye and simply say "Thank you."

Q. Why don't Asha and Saundra have any close female friends?

A. Well, Asha doesn't have any close friends of either gender because she doesn't really trust anyone but herself. Saundra has Evelyn but she is also one of those women who prefer that their male lover fill the role of confidant. I'm not saying that Saundra is right—it is simply a lifestyle choice. Also, with both these young women, MOTHER is a major unresolved issue. Can you really have deep female friendships if you are angry at your own mother? I really don't know.

Q. Is *The Other Side of The Game* a message novel?

A. No. I don't set out to write "message" novels because they usually bore the hell out of the reader. However, by the time I'd finished writing this book, it was clear to me that its theme had something to do with our inability to see our parents as flawed, three-dimensional people. We prefer to keep them in a romanticized cage called "nurturer" and not notice any unfulfilled yearnings they have or forgive them the mistakes they have made.

Q. Will there be a sequel?

A. Yes. Nick certainly has his hands full as he tries to mold Asha into the perfect wife. He will want her to be an elegant, well-bred lady by day and a whore in his bed at night. In the sequel, entitled *Denzel's Lips*, readers will watch Nick flail about trying to change another human being. We'll see.

THE OTHER SIDE OF THE GAME

ANITA DOREEN DIGGS

ABOUT THIS GUIDE

The questions and discussion topics that follow are
intended to enhance your group's reading of
this book. We hope they provide new insights and ways of
looking at this wonderful novel.

DISCUSSION QUESTIONS

1. Anita Doreen Diggs has gained a loyal following for her characters like Adrienne (*A Mighty Love*) and Jacqueline (*A Meeting in the Ladies' Room*) who come from poor or working class backgrounds. Is this a return to realism in Black fiction after more than a decade of upper class, highly educated female characters?

2. Discuss what Adrienne, Jacqueline, Asha, and Saundra all have in common.

   What do you think these similarities say about the author?

3. In what ways do we see the heartrending legacy of Asha's father at work in her relationship with Nick, Brent, and Randall?

4. How do Saundra's feelings about Asha change over the course of the novel?

5. Why is Asha jealous of Saundra and how does she show it?

6. Where do you see Asha, Saundra, Phil, Hugo and Evelyn five years after the close of the novel? Do you think Phil and Saundra will ever be close again?

7. Is Asha a more honest person than Saundra? Why?

8. Was Phil a good father? What more could he or should he have given his only child?

9. Why did Asha cheat on Nick? Will she do it again?

10. How did Evelyn contribute to her own heartbreak? How long should a woman wait for a man to commit?

Dear Reader,

Greetings from Harlem! I hope you've enjoyed *The Other Side of the Game* and will take the time to read *A Mighty Love* and *A Meeting in the Ladies' Room,* both of which have heroines who fight against tremendous odds on the road to happiness.

I've just completed my fourth novel, a story of sex, stardom, and success. It's called *Denzel's Lips,* and it will be published by Kensington Books in Fall 2006. If you'd like to be added to my mailing list, please send your name and home or e-mail address to Glamourwins@aol.com.

Lastly, to learn more about my activities and personal appearances, go to my Web site, www.anitadoreendiggs.com.

Thanks for your continued support!
Anita Doreen Diggs